Being Li£

Helen Smith lives in Brixton with her daughter

Also by Helen Smith
Alison Wonderland

Being Light

Helen Smith

VICTOR GOLLANCZ
LONDON

First published in Great Britain
in 1999 by Orion
An imprint of Orion Books Ltd
Orion House, 5 Upper St Martin's Lane,
London WC2H 9EA

A CIP catalogue record for this book
is available from the British Library

ISBN 0 575 07093 5

Typeset in Great Britain by Deltatype Ltd, Birkenhead, Wirral

This book proof printed by
Antony Rowe Ltd, Chippenham, Wiltshire

This book is for my parents

Acknowledgements

With thanks to Christine Kidney and Caroline Dawnay

1

The Castle

Roy Travers and his friend Brian Donald begin setting up the bouncy castle in Brockwell Park early in the morning, while the light is still weak and they are only half awake. It's a very windy day in late April, with a light drizzle forecast for this afternoon, but they and the other volunteers are expecting a large crowd to turn out from midday to raise money for St Thomas's Hospital Scanner Appeal.

The bouncy castle, lent to them for the occasion by a local business, is the star attraction for the younger children, together with the pony rides. It is very shiny, made from an expensive prototype material of the kind that is primarily used in modern metallic stay-fresh crisp packets.

'Funny weather for a fun day,' says Brian, who has no gift for observational humour. Roy ignores him, crouched inside the bouncy castle at the back, patting and smoothing the walls to make sure it is inflated correctly. The inflation is just right. They have made the walls and the turrets of the castle fat and sausagey without putting a strain on the material.

Brian hunches over a Silk Cut Ultra Mild with his disposable lighter, his back turned against the wind, hoping to reward himself with a quick smoke before checking that the guy ropes are secure. His wife doesn't like him smoking. She was the one who told the Hospital Fundraising Committee he would be prepared to spend his day off buggering about with the bouncy castle, so he doesn't feel too bad.

The wind nudges the castle. The ground is soft because it has been raining. The metal pegs slide from the earth like hungry fingers through custard. The castle bumps an inch or two along the ground, trailing the guy ropes. Unheeding, Brian flicks at his lighter and makes a windshield for the cigarette with the lapel of his jacket, turning his back one way and then another against the intensifying wind, whipping around him from all directions.

With the persistence and strength of an elephant moving tree trunks in the jungle, the wind produces a fierce, blowing burst that transforms the anchorless castle into a flying craft, Roy Travers its only passenger.

At first Roy laughs as he feels it lift beneath him. Bouncy castles are usually a bit tame as an amusement, except for the smallest children, but a flyaway castle strikes him as funny for a few seconds as it rises swiftly on the strong spurt of wind.

'Hey,' Roy shouts, as much to the castle as to anyone else, as if it might come to its senses and deposit him back on the ground. Brian runs after him and tries, and fails, to catch hold of the guy ropes to bring him back to earth. Perhaps he'd have made more of an effort if they had winning lottery tickets pinned to them.

Neither Roy nor Brian have been involved in a tragedy before, although they sometimes watch the drama documentaries on the BBC that re-create real life rescues, with many of those involved self-consciously playing themselves. Unfortunately, like so many amateurs in tragedies of this kind, Roy and Brian have no sense of occasion and as a consequence they fail to act quickly or appropriately. They both assume that the flying bouncy castle will drift back to earth. Brian takes out his camera and snaps a few photos. The bouncy castle climbs higher and higher, the wind keeping it aloft skilfully as if harnessing the gentle hands of an invisible juggling circus troupe.

Roy crawls to the front of the castle on his knees, holds on, looks down. He tries to overcome his fear of heights. He has to jump from the castle and save himself. He raises himself to a standing position, knees slightly bent to keep his balance, still holding on. The castle has risen high enough in the air to brush tree tops. How tall are trees? Ten feet? Twelve? Fifteen? Roy tries to visualize himself standing on Brian Donald's shoulders. Would he be able to reach out and touch the tree tops? How tall is a first-floor window? If you jump from the first floor, do you survive? The castle continues to climb. What about the chances of survival if you jump from a second-floor window?

Roy returns to a crouching position, then moves again to get comfortable, resting his weight on his knees, holding on, looking down. He is too dangerously far from the ground to risk a jump. He switches his focus to remaining on the castle, as if it were his saviour rather than his captor. He finds a reasonably comfortable position, half reclining like a Roman guest at a feast, his feet jammed into a pocket in one of the side walls, his hands gripping the material beneath him. He feels secure enough to appreciate, if not actually enjoy, the view of the English countryside as he sails above it.

With the quietness, the wind in his hair, the gentle bobbing motion of the castle, Roy could almost believe himself lost at sea if it weren't for the scenery below. In a rustic tableau reminiscent of an earlier, more innocent age, he sees a mother with two children on bicycles in a country lane. They wave at him as he floats overhead. What is the correct response? He has no materials to make a placard and spell out 'Help'. The tiny figures are too far below him to read his distress in hand signals. Unwilling to disappoint the children, he waves tentatively. Still the flying castle climbs. The air is very cold. He wishes he could sail nearer the sun, so he could feel its warmth.

Roy loses track of the passage of time. He feels himself becoming light-headed as the air grows thinner. The prototype bouncy castle material, subject to unpredicted changes in temperature, begins to shrink. Roy lifts his lolling head and squints at the sun, trying to assess whether there is a danger of sailing too near and shrinking his craft enough to plummet him to the earth. His last thoughts are of his wife as, eyes tightly shut, he feels the material beneath him wrinkle and contract, hears the menacing hiss of the air inside escaping, feels the too-quick descent towards earth and certain death.

Roy has heard that if you don't wake up when you feel yourself falling as you go to sleep at night, you will die. Dying and falling are indistinguishable for Roy in his final moments. He wakes in the arms of an angel. She isn't beautiful, although she is wearing white and she's soft and comforting. 'Well,' she says. 'Well, well, well. Welcome to Paradise.'

2

Personne Disparue

Sheila Travers reports Roy's disappearance the next day, calling in to Brixton police station to file the information in person.

'You have to wait forty-eight hours before you can file a missing person report,' the desk sergeant tells her.

'It isn't a straightforward missing person report. It's an accident report. An incident report.' Sheila picks at the bobbles on her coat, looking down. Then she looks the sergeant straight in the eye. 'Please, I need to know whether a body has been found.'

The desk sergeant checks his computer screen and reassures her that Roy's body hasn't been found.

'What kind of man is your husband?'

The question seems a strange one. It strikes Sheila as being unnecessarily intrusive. It carries the implication that Roy's personality could have some sort of bearing on the outcome of his freak accident, which is impossible. 'Roy is a sensible man.'

The sergeant, following Sheila's troubled reaction to his question in the frown lines on her face, seems relieved by the answer when she finally gives it. 'Well, then. Wherever he has landed, he will try to make his way back home. Why don't you go back there and wait? I'm sure you'll hear something from him soon.'

Sheila waits for him for over a week, starting at every sound outside her front door in case it is Roy without his key; lifting the phone receiver every so often to check the dialling tone; not eating properly; not going out in case there is some news; switching on the kettle to make tea and then not making it, switching it on again, letting it boil; switching every switch in the house and switching them all off again.

On the following Monday, with no sign of Roy and still no body found, Sheila decides she needs to enlist the help of all available agencies, including unconventional ones. She visits a clairvoyant in a pleasant, airy flat in Josephine Avenue, off Brixton Hill. The visit is a first for Sheila, although strictly speaking she is no stranger to the supernatural. When she was nine years old, she and her friends watched as a very bright, elliptical light hovered above their heads as they walked home from the school bus stop in the winter darkness. The likelihood of alien life forms drawing near to study the tiny figures in red and grey uniforms was debated in the junior school for weeks. It is the only other time in her life that Sheila has been prepared to believe that there might be more in this world than whatever she can see on the surface but the incident is half-buried in the mythology of Sheila's childhood and she hasn't thought about it for more than thirty years.

Sheila has never written to a magazine for advice, never taken part in a documentary for Channel Four, never believed in her horoscope (although she reads it) and never, ever turned to the spirit world for guidance. Now something outside the ordinary has happened to Roy and Sheila needs someone outside the ordinary to provide a clue to Roy's continuing absence, as the police cannot. Sheila sets aside her misgivings and sounds the buzzer for the flat in Josephine Avenue.

The clairvoyant's name is Dorothy. She's in her late thirties, has badly bitten fingernails, an expensive feathered haircut and ever so slightly too-tight trousers. Her flat smells of air freshener but her manner is reassuring.

Dorothy takes the photograph of Roy being blown away on the bouncy castle, thoughtfully passed on to Sheila by Brian Donald, and rests her hands on it in her lap, closing her eyes. Seconds pass. Long seconds, running into minutes. Sheila is embarrassed and impressed by the silence, unsure whether to fill it. From the kitchen, she can distinctly hear the sound of Dorothy's cat eating its dry food supplement from the plastic bowl on the linoleum.

'I see him floating,' says Dorothy at last. 'I see him floating.' She settles back, easing the pressure caused by sitting upright in the trousers, apparently prepared to let the matter rest. Sheila tries to pin Dorothy down to an interpretation of this information.

'On a boat?'

'Perhaps.'

'On a river or on the sea?'

'The sea?' The inflection in Dorothy's voice suggests participation in a parlour guessing game rather than the insight of an all-seeing oracle.

The minimal information Sheila gathers in this consultation with Dorothy strongly indicates to her that the wind has taken Roy across the Channel. What other stretch of sea could have transported him to a land mass quickly enough for him to have survived the journey? It is extremely fortunate that she has been collecting tokens from the *Daily Mail* to exchange for a ferry ticket to France for only one pound, as this will enable her to travel inexpensively to look for him there.

'One more thing, Sheila. I can see him standing on a

platform, preparing to step off. It's a very vivid picture. I don't know what it means.'

Sheila spends Tuesday and Wednesday with a French dictionary, paper, pens, glue and scissors. By Thursday she's ready to go to Calais to search for Roy, one of only a few foot passengers to make the trip. Most of her fellow travellers are bootleggers in cars or vans, making a round trip to Calais to buy bottles of Jacob's Creek at prices which offer a considerable saving compared to current deals in British supermarkets and off-licences.

Fifteen minutes into the journey, Sheila starts to feel sick. Her weakened body is powerless to stop anxious thoughts crowding her mind. Where is Roy? What's become of him? She clings to the hope that he's alive. Sheila cannot and will not believe that Roy is dead. She holds tight to the rail of the ferry, pea green and sick, not with the motion of the boat but with the effort of disbelieving the evidence of his disappearance. He cannot be dead. He would not have left her. She must believe in him. Believing will give her the strength to bring him back, wherever he has gone, or been taken. Alone, sick, frightened, Sheila spaces her feet a little apart on the wooden deck of the ferry to keep her balance as the boat rocks with the movement of the sea in the middle of the English Channel. She's determined to believe.

Sheila has a thin stack of home-made A3-sized posters with her, photocopied in the local newsagent's, each with a photograph of Roy. The words ask for help from the French people in their own language: 'Personne Disparue. Est-ce que vous avez vu cette personne?'

Standing on the ferry, attempting to create a reality in which Roy is still alive and trying to get back home, Sheila tries to transmit her belief in him to wherever he is, so that he will know and take comfort. She reaches into her nylon travelling bag and takes out the posters to look at his blurry likeness, enlarged and photocopied from a holiday snapshot. The wind tugs at the topmost poster and whips it out of her hands, flinging the paper against the rail before snatching it up again, toying with it and then dashing it down into the waves. Sheila stuffs the rest of the posters back into her bag, not watching.

Once she reaches Calais, Sheila glues the posters all around the town. The day is exhausting and disappointing. In attending to the detail of creating the posters and buying a ferry ticket, Sheila hasn't paid attention to the overall strategy of the plan. Now that she has arrived in France, she feels daunted by the scope of her search. She feels useless and frustrated and foolish. She has no idea how to generate leads or gather information. She walks round and round and tries to talk to people, without learning any news of Roy. At the end of a disappointing day, Sheila goes into the hypermarché to buy some cheese and wine before catching the last ferry home. She hopes that shopping will provide some solace because it is normal and everyday but the lights in the hypermarché are so bright that they give her a headache and, as she takes a trolley from the rack, out of the corner of her eye she sees the doors of a lift close on a man who has been too slow to get out of it, trapping his arm.

The day after her return to England, Sheila visits the clairvoyant again.

'I think he's in a happier place,' Dorothy tells Sheila, with tears in her eyes. Sheila pays the clairvoyant the money for the consultation but she won't believe her. She goes back to the flat to wait for him.

Perhaps Roy is being held somewhere against his will, unable to get back home? A few days after his disappearance Sheila came across an advertisement in the local paper which she pinned to the noticeboard in the kitchen, although she hoped she wouldn't need it:

FITZGERALD'S BUREAU OF INVESTIGATIONS
— DISCRETION ASSURED

It seems that the time has come to seek help from these people. When Sheila telephones, it is Mrs Fitzgerald herself who answers. She sounds sympathetic and experienced. Sheila makes an appointment to meet Mrs Fitzgerald and another woman named Alison, who will be assigned to help her look for Roy. For the first time since he disappeared, Sheila feels that she has got some help from people who know what they're doing.

3

On the Bus

Ella Fitzgerald is riding the buses again. She has found this an excellent opportunity to observe mad people who ride around all day long on a Travelcard, mumbling to themselves. Today she has selected the 159, one of the few services that still uses the hop-on hop-off Routemaster buses with conductors. She has travelled from Brixton to Oxford Circus and is now on her way back home again.

Looking through the windows of the top deck of the bus, she can see a silvery, shimmery bright sun. I must learn to see the world the way others see it, she thinks. There is something fanciful about the way I see things and I have to stop. Everyone knows the sun is gold or yellow. Even very young children know it, if you look at their drawings. I've always seen the sun as silver. If I can learn to see that colour as yellow, I'll be like other people. I'll be normal.

Mrs Fitzgerald is thinking about madness. More than anything else, more than poverty or war or assaults from local teenagers, Mrs Fitzgerald fears going mad like her brother. What are the signs? She hopes to learn from her fellow passengers.

When she looks outside again, as the bus pulls out of

Lambeth Road and turns right towards Kennington, the world seems to have gone wrong. Her position at the front of the bus on the top deck gives her an excellent 270-degree vantage point. There to her left, as it should be, is the Imperial War Museum, formerly Bedlam. In front of the bus, behind the bus, all around the bus, there is a sea of people as far as she can see. Most are walking but some are on bicycles. It's impossible to tell whether the atmosphere is jolly or menacing. It has something of a carnival feel, which usually means a mixture of both. Mrs Fitzgerald can hear booming music and the shrill, discordant sound from whistles strung round people's necks on coloured strings, jammed in their mouths, blowing at full volume.

'Reclaim London' is written on home-made banners waving above the crowds. Mrs Fitzgerald has the sudden, icy fear that these are mad people, spilling out from Bedlam, reclaiming the capital city and taking her with them as one of them. Looking around the bus, she sees she's quite alone on the top deck. There are enough people outside to pick up the bus and carry it along on their shoulders, Mrs Fitzgerald above them like some carnival queen of the mad people. Is it possible that they *know*? Is she so like them that they can sense that she sees the sun as silver? 'The sun is yellow, the sun is yellow, the sun is yellow,' chants Mrs Fitzgerald, seizing on the thing that will make her normal and different from them. 'The sun is yellow, the sunny's yellow, the sunnys yellow, sunnys yellow, sunnys yellow, sunnysyellow.'

The conductor lays a gentle hand on her shoulder. God, there are so many disturbed people on the bus these days, he should get a care worker's allowance. The conductor's fingers smell faintly of the grease from the roast chicken sandwiches he has been eating from their tinfoil wrapper a moment before. 'It's a demo, love. Anti-traffic, anti-vehicles. Bloody cyclists. They think they own London. You might be better slipping off the

bus and taking the Tube. You can stay if you want, though.'
Sometimes they just like somewhere warm to sit.

Mrs Fitzgerald, dry-mouthed, cannot bring herself to reply.
Outside, head and shoulders above the other demonstrators, a
beautiful blond young man balances on the pedals of a unicycle.
He's wearing a dress. He holds his hand up to the bus driver
through the open sliding door that gives access to the driver's
seat. The driver keeps it open against regulations because he
thinks it looks cool. The demonstrator's hand, palm up, loose at
the wrist, looks like a foppish invitation to the bus driver to
dance. He wakes up all his muscles at once and lunges from the
unicycle, pulling the driver from his seat and taking his place
behind the wheel, the bus engine still idling.

Jeremy grips the wheel, his hands in position at ten to two,
leaning forward slightly, mastering the great machine. He moves
the gear lever on the shaft below the over-sized wheel into first
gear and the bus edges forward, slowly. The protesters fall back,
whistling and jeering. Jeremy clips the pedals of the cyclists on
the near side of the road as he adjusts to steering the
unfamiliarly wide vehicle.

Routemaster buses are semi-automatic. There is no clutch.
The drivers slip into neutral and rev the engine before changing
gear. Jeremy fails to do this. The bus lurches and comes to a halt
two hundred yards further down the road, where the driver
pulls Jeremy from the bus by his hair and regains his seat.

The psychic postman stands at Alison's door, patiently feeding
birthday cards through the letterbox. Thirty years old. She hides
from view, does not feel like talking.

'Alison,' calls the postman, his lips to the letterbox. 'Are you
allright?'

'I'm frumpy, overweight, dog tired, smelling of milk, vomit,
piss and Bonjela.'

13

'Oh.'

'But it's OK. I'm slowly climbing out of the pit.'

'It might be post-natal depression. You should see someone about it.' A plume of his cigarette smoke reaches Alison through the letterbox. The postman's concern is touching. She presses her thumb and forefinger into the inner corner of each eye, using pressure to stop the tears the way first-aiders stop blood seeping from a small wound.

Alison's daughter, Phoebe, is around a year old now. Alison isn't sure of Phoebe's exact age because she found the baby at the seaside last summer. While there is general sympathy these days for women who suffer from post-natal depression, Alison is aware there would be little sympathy left to go round for women who have found a baby and kept it.

One of Alison's birthday cards is home-made. It has a pressed cornflower on the front and a cutting from a newspaper inside, telling the story of a young child with defective vision who saw tiny particles of dust in the air magnified many times and thought they were fairies floating in front of her eyes. Optometrists corrected the child's sight by giving her rose-coloured glasses to wear.

The card is from Jeff, Alison's former downstairs neighbour. He's moved a long way away in the hope of forgetting her. The card suggests he's having some difficulty with this.

Alison takes out a postcard of one of Picasso's portraits of a woman with a messed up head, bought on a visit to the Museum of Modern Art in New York, and writes a simple message to the return address:

My hands are rough, my lips are chapped. I'm 30, I feel old.
Help me.

Alison creeps up to the cot in the next room where Phoebe is having a nap. The child's arms are thrown back and bent up at the elbow like a 1930s strongman, knees and toes turned out and her head to one side. Alison bends into the cot to watch for movement behind Phoebe's long eyelashes and bluish eyelids as she sleeps. There's a sudden deep, reassuring sleepy breath from the baby, and Alison steps back and turns away.

Harvey is sitting in his room in the fading light, hands tucked under his thighs, leaning forward, tensed. He looks like a track athlete practising for a new set of rules that requires competitors to start each race from a sitting position on the sofa.

Harvey's eyes are closed, searching inward for his earliest memories of himself. He was a weedy child, popular with other children's mothers because of his beautiful manners. Harvey remembers trying for the first time to grasp the meaning of the events that surrounded and involved him. It was while he was at school in the seventies, during an era when it was more fashionable to allow children to discover the great truths for themselves than to explain anything to them, that Harvey first tried to make sense of the world. He did this by paying attention to the labels given to everything and everyone by other people.

Harvey is examining memories of shivering in a purple cotton matching vest and pants set in PE at primary school, fighting among the scaled down toilets in the infant block, queuing for school dinners, winding string round pillow cases and leaving them overnight in buckets of coloured water, twisting elastic round his legs then jumping high and clear of it. All these activities were unfathomable.

Harvey remembers the morning he and the rest of his class spent their time folding scratchy pieces of paper very small and snipping at them with scissors with rounded ends. 'You've made a snowflake,' the teacher told him. The information gave him some comfort, even though it was a palpable untruth. Once one of the activities had been named he could ask for it again, or avoid it, or measure it against other things with the same name.

It was only in his nightmares, or under the bed, or behind the curtains in the dark that shapeless frightening things remained, still unnamed.

A phone call brings Harvey back from the darkness and he opens his eyes.

'Your advertising campaigns for cars are very successful.'

'Well, thank you. I can't really take the credit. I'm a hired hand – part of a creative team. I'm sorry, I don't think I recognise your voice.'

'Mine is a lone voice roaring in a concrete jungle.'

'Yes?'

'Do you know what cars are doing to this planet?'

'Who are you?'

'I'm the one who's going to make you see that you are wrong. I'm going to stop the traffic.'

Harvey walks upstairs to Alison.

'Do you know what cars are doing to this planet?'

'The lead in the petrol makes children stupid. Cars clutter up the streets and knock cyclists off their bikes. The fumes from the exhaust turn the buildings black and they wither the trees at the side of the road. Ask Taron, she goes out morning, noon and night to try and revive the trees.'

'Do you ever feel like campaigning for a cause?'

'No. Causes are for students, politicians and the childless.'

Harvey lives in Alison's basement. He likes to talk to her about the need to define and label everything in his life.

'If something doesn't have a name, how can it *be*?' he asks. 'If you've never heard something described or named, how can you know you want it? How can you be sure you've ever experienced it? Once you've given something a name, you've captured it and made something constant in an inconstant world.'

'Like naming stars?' asks Alison.

'Naming stars doesn't count. They're intangible, too far away. It would be like naming particles of dust. It doesn't contribute anything to our experience of the world.'

'I think naming stars is cute.'

'Yes, it's cute, but it doesn't affect anyone except the person who's named it. No one would ever see the star and wonder what it was called. The whole thing is too remote from our normal world.'

'What about feelings? They're intangible.'

'Describing feelings is different than naming stars. Feelings influence the way everyone acts and so they make the world the way it is. But I've often wondered, if you don't have a name for a feeling, then maybe you don't feel it. There's a word in Welsh, *hiraeth*, that's like homesickness but it's stronger, it evokes a kind of national pride as well. I don't think English people feel that word. The thing is, if the word existed in English, would it increase the range of people's feelings? Would some people feel like that?'

'Are you saying that if you don't know about something then you can't feel it?'

'Maybe. If you don't know a place exists, how can you know you want to go there? If you'd never heard about New York, if it wasn't even called by any name, how would you know how exciting it was? Once a few people have come back and said, "You must go to New York, it is a city that never sleeps," you know you will go there eventually.'

'Maybe that's why so many people feel so lost. There's a place they should be, but they don't know it exists or where it is or how to get there. Do you ever feel that you're adrift, Harvey?'

'Yes. I don't know whether you should try to make sense of

the small things around you or understand the bigger picture. I dither between the two approaches. I sometimes think the key is to try to convert every unknown thing into something I know and understand.'

'What is it about the unknown that bothers you so much?'

'I think I want everything around me to be solid to stop that drifting feeling you're talking about. Maybe I'm just worried about missing out on something. Imagine if there's life after death, for example. There could be a great big decadent party going on in Heaven and we're all grimly clinging on to life, with scientists finding ways for people to live longer and longer.'

'I know what you mean. I drove for ages on the A3 once expecting it to turn into the M3 and it never did. It's that horror of being stuck on a dual carriageway when you could be whizzing along on the motorway.'

'Yes. If I know as much as possible about everything then every choice I make will be informed. I just don't know how I can go about making sure that I know everything. I'm not doing much about it at the moment. I spend my days going to the gym and hanging out with Jane Memory, in between doing a bit of freelance work.'

'I wonder if we're all just dribbling our lives away.'

'No. Some people live valiantly. Someone called me up just now, someone I don't know, and told me he was going to stop the traffic. I keep thinking about it. He sounded so certain that he could do it.'

'You were contacted by a voice from the unknown?'

'Yes.'

'With some sort of plan that could change your life?'

'Apparently.'

'Do you think that was maybe your one chance to live valiantly?'

'I didn't see it like that at the time. I just put the phone down.

Anyway, I don't want to live valiantly, I want to live knowing I haven't missed out on the party being thrown by all the other people who are living valiantly.'

4

Heaven and Earth

Roy's a little disappointed, although not surprised, to find that life in Heaven is similar to life on Earth. The air is purer, the scenery lovelier, the stars brighter but otherwise it's pretty much the same.

Roy thought Heaven would be crowded with all the other people who have already died but there are no buildings other than the one he lives in and no one around except Sylvia, the angel who caught him as he fell. He wonders if Heaven is different for each person. He has plenty of time for reflection now that he doesn't have a job to go to. Perhaps you get what suits you. On Earth, he wasn't sociable, he was always happy just spending time with his wife. Here in Heaven he also has one constant companion – Sylvia.

Sylvia lives in a stone farmhouse with cool white sheets on the bed and a warm kitchen that always smells of bread. She keeps some chickens, ducks, a cow, a dog and an elephant. There's a vegetable garden, a flower garden and an orchard. Roy walks out every day and explores his patch of Heaven. It is bordered on three sides by the sea. If he walks inland for about forty-five minutes, there's a small white fence with a hand-painted sign that says 'Paradise'.

Time is the one thing that is endless in Heaven, stretching forward into infinity. It is impossible to imagine beginnings or endings. The days are long, uncluttered by work, unpunctuated by television or radio, by visits from friends or trips to the supermarket. Time is a luxury but it is also awesomely powerful and endless. Every day that ends promises another just like it tomorrow. There's a sense of power in being able to change the day just by doing some small thing differently, by preparing something different for dinner, by starting a conversation on a new subject matter, by walking in a different direction to the sign on the wooden fence. Waking up in the morning and looking at the blank canvas of the day, for Roy, is like looking at the ocean and contemplating the infinitesimal changes and understanding the timelessness and the not-sameness, the endless variations on being an ocean. Perhaps the physical limits of the Heaven that Roy and Sylvia inhabit are restricted because restriction enhances the ability to comprehend infinity.

Sylvia pads about comfortably and talks only when she needs to communicate something to Roy, she isn't a chatty person. Roy isn't surprised that Sylvia speaks English, or if she doesn't speak English, that in dying he's been given the facility to understand the language they speak in Heaven. Roy doesn't talk to Sylvia about Heaven or what it feels like to be here. The one thing he's curious about is what kind of life she used to live.

'In my old life, I trained animals for film and TV work. My hero was Rolf Knie, the humane animal trainer. He taught elephants to ride a scooter, climb stairs on their hind legs and use a typewriter. He made history in nineteen forty-one by training an elephant to walk the tightrope. He was so famous that Princess Margaret was in the audience when he brought his elephants to London in the early nineteen fifties. My dream was to train an elephant to walk the tightrope. I was always kind to the animals but I know now that it's wrong.'

'Why is it wrong, if you were kind?'

'Because we were displaying the animals for entertainment. It was wrong. I read a report about it a few years ago that completely changed my life.'

'Well, I used to do something similar. I used to work in a kennels where we bred and trained dogs. They lived like kings. They had everything. There was no cruelty, it was all done on reward. Mrs Latimer was very careful about that.'

'Mrs Latimer?'

'Yes.'

'Mrs Latimer, who controls the supply of performing dogs to the film and circus industries?'

'Yes.'

'Roy, I don't think we should talk about our other lives, before we came here.'

Although there are no other human people in Heaven with Roy and Sylvia, she has been joined by some of her friends from the animal kingdom. Maybe Sylvia doesn't need to talk about her old life because she's surrounded by mementos. An elderly dog lives in the house with her and an elephant sleeps in one of two hangar-sized barns in the garden. The other barn stores the elephant's supply of hay.

Roy has looked around for his old dead friends, in case they've been waiting here for him. There's no one and it's made him realise that he didn't really have anyone. He thinks sometimes about whether his wife will turn up one day but it makes him uncomfortable. How would Sylvia deal with the situation?

Possibly he's overestimating the likelihood of seeing Sheila again. His wife was always very fond of the theatre, perhaps she'll go to a thespian Heaven. It seems strange that, now it turns out there is an afterlife, he might not spend eternity with her. If there had been nothing after death, he could have accepted it. But this scattered eternity . . . At least he recognizes there's no point in arguing with Sylvia.

'OK,' he says. 'Let's not talk about it.' Having come to terms early on with the theological difficulties of making love to an angel, Roy takes Sylvia's hand and they go to bed at the end of a day that promises another just like it tomorrow.

Brian Donald's wife has sent him round to the flat in Brixton after work this evening to see if Sheila Travers is all right. Brian's wife is at home looking after her bedridden mother so she can't go herself. She's worried because she can't get any answer from Sheila on the phone and Sheila hasn't returned any of her messages.

Brian has always been a bit wary of Sheila. She is a quiet person, with a determination and depth to her personality that he has always shied away from, associating that kind of quiet certainty with people who suddenly become born-again Christians.

Brian and his wife and his wife's mother saw a local news item recently about a man whose solar-powered roof panels generate more than enough electricity for his own house so that he has been able to sell some of it back to his local Electricity Board. The story reminded Brian of Roy and Sheila. They formed a happy unit together, as if they didn't need anyone else. They were so solid together and generated so much happiness as a couple that Sheila persuaded Roy that they had more than enough for themselves and should give something back, which is why they helped out with fundraising at charitable events.

Brian's wife wondered sometimes why Roy and Sheila had never had children but it was not the sort of conversation Brian would have been comfortable having with Roy. He couldn't see a gap in Roy and Sheila's lives that would have been filled by children. His own son, twenty years old and incapable of doing his own laundry, is still living at home.

Since Roy's disappearance Brian and his wife have been wondering about the dark secrets Roy and Sheila's life must have held. They turned the television off so they could spend the evening discussing it. Brian himself saw Roy float up on the bouncy castle. It couldn't have travelled far. Roy has either had a bump on the head or he staged the whole thing and he's run off with someone else. Brian's mother-in-law suggested that Sheila's capable manner hides a sexual coldness that drove Roy away. Brian's wife thought Roy might have gambling debts. Brian wondered whether Roy had fled the country to be a sexual tourist in Thailand.

Brian will ask Sheila if he can have a look at Roy's passport, which will put to rest whether or not he has gone abroad. Brian's wife told him to buy Sheila a bunch of flowers to cheer her up but he hasn't bought any in case she isn't in. Also, Brian has never been alone in her home with Sheila before. He feels a bit uncomfortable about it under the circumstances, especially if she is sexually cold. He can always pop out and get the flowers later.

Brian rings the doorbell. When there is no answer, he shouts her name through the letterbox. He's not sure whether she would hear him as she lives on the second floor, but at least he can tell his wife that he tried. If Sheila is not in, he can use the ten pounds his wife gave him for the flowers for something else. If he puts it on a horse and it wins, he will take his wife out for the evening. Their son can look after his grandmother for a change.

Sheila can see Brian Donald from her window. She has nothing whatsoever to say to him. He is well-intentioned but he would have nothing to say that she would want to hear. He would rattle the coins in his pockets, rise up and down on the balls of his feet and stare at her breasts. Sheila does not answer the door.

5

The Message

Jane Memory is scratching the inside of her right nostril with the rubber on the end of a pencil, briefing the stylist on her mobile phone. 'The theme is empire builders. I need a great photo to go with this piece. Hold on to empire. See what you can do with it.'

Jane Memory knows lots of people and phones them all the time to maintain her network. She's popular because she's funny, although she has a very critical eye. Every time she attends a dinner party in an unfamiliar house she murmurs a style-mag appraisal of it without stopping to think whether she's offending her host. Jane is hungry all the time and the hunger makes her irritable and sometimes rather unkind. She's hungry because she's very thin, it's her thing. She doesn't even take slimming pills, she relies on willpower to resist the foods that pile on the millimetres.

Venetia Latimer sits where the stylist has left her, on a wooden kitchen chair in the middle of the photographer's studio. She has a maroon silk turban on her head, with a cameo brooch clipped to the front. Her body is swathed in emerald silk fashioned into an extravagant fifties-style dress, the plunging neckline edged in seed pearls exposing the cleft of her bosom.

Two Dalmations stand very still against her glimmering skirt while the photographs are taken. There are so many bracelets on her arm that after careful study of the contact sheets the next day, the photographer will fancy he can still hear them chiming.

Roy would come back home, if he could. It is the one unarguable fact in Sheila Travers' life. Why would he not come back? She has an unshakeable faith in Roy's compulsion to find his way home, as if he were a spawning salmon and south London a sparkling stream. She is alone in this; even her own family are beginning to doubt she will see her husband again soon.

'Sheila, maybe Roy has lost his memory? Or perhaps,' Sheila's sister faces the inevitable on her behalf, 'perhaps he's not alive.'

'I'm sure he's alive.'

Given that Roy's will to come back is a constant, everything else Sheila has ever believed is negotiable. Sitting in her finery in the upper circle of the Palace Theatre with her sister, trying to take her mind off Roy's disappearance, Sheila receives a message about him.

'Do you mean someone passed you a note?' Sheila's sister is bewildered when Sheila tries to explain as they sip their pre-ordered interval drinks. 'I saw nothing.'

'It wasn't a note. It was a message that went directly into my head.'

'The voice of God?' Sheila's sister's lips are drawn very tightly over her teeth and her eyes are small. She disapproves of religious experiences very strongly indeed.

'Oh, it wasn't the voice of God. I've always expected that to be like an announcement over a tannoy system, very loud and slightly distorted. It was more like telepathy. I didn't hear words, even. I just reached an understanding.'

'Which is?'

'He's been abducted. He can't come back because he isn't free. Someone has taken him.'

Tickets for West End shows are expensive. Sheila's sister bought them as a treat to try and cheer up. The two women sit through the rest of the play. Sheila's sister is furious because Sheila distracts her, sitting and fiddling with her earrings as if tuning them in to some Mayday frequency from outer space. 'Come in, Lieutenant Uhuru,' she says when she recounts the story to her husband that night, mimicking Sheila to make him laugh and relieve some of the tension she's feeling.

Back at her flat with a cup of tea, Sheila wonders whether there was something special that allowed the message to get through. Were her earrings acting as some sort of aerial?

6

Sylvia

Sylvia Arrow is humming 'It's raining men' as she kneads the day's supply of bread. Sylvia was a high-wire artiste in her youth, but her hips and thighs broadened as she reached her twenties. She has the kind of body that will always be strong and flexible but she became too heavy to perform professionally. Sylvia remained with the circus for a while, the only life she knew, grounded but content, knitting spangly bikini costumes for the other girls, using very fine gauge needles.

When she grew tired of the performers teasing her about her doughy limbs and pinching her arms and legs to make red dots in the white flesh, Sylvia ran away from the circus. She left behind the only person she'd ever loved, a boy whose superficial resemblance to herself meant Sylvia treated him like a brother, whispering him stories from where she sat knitting in her deckchair as he rested between performances as an acrobat in the big top.

For five years Sylvia worked as a croupier, salting away the pay and dreaming about the circus. For five more years, Sylvia trained animals, working for the undisputed expert in the field, Venetia Latimer. Then she ran away from that life too. Sylvia's name is a reminder of the very early days; she chose it for herself when she went into show business. As she flew in the air, spinning above people in the big top, Sylvia had a vision in her head that she was shining and metallic and swift and hard like a silver arrow. The other reminder is the high wire and the net she stretches in the garden sometimes, just to practise, for old times' sake. It was as well for Roy she was feeling sentimental the day he flew overhead because the net probably saved him from breaking his neck as he fell.

In her twenties, Sylvia sometimes thought she didn't need sex if she could eat fresh bread every day instead. In her late thirties, with cupboards full of flour and yeast, the time and patience to bake every day, and a man who has dropped from the skies to be her companion, Sylvia is pleasantly surprised to find she doesn't even have to choose any more.

Mrs Fitzgerald is at home with a cup of black coffee. It is late but she is still working, straining her eyes as she bends over the paper trail she has amassed in her latest investigation into animal welfare.

Animal welfare is of such great interest to young people in Britain that it has been estimated that at any given time, up to fifteen per cent of casual workers in zoos and circuses are undercover agents working for animal rights organizations. Although the elaborate concealment of fragile miniature video cameras can occasionally restrict their capacity for heavy work, the majority of them can make themselves useful with a spade. Given declining ticket sales, it's doubtful whether the zoos and circuses could survive without the contribution made by these young people.

Following her seminal report about the circus industry, published to wide acclaim ten years ago and credited with being in part responsible for growing public distaste at the spectacle of performing animals, Mrs Fizgerald is acknowleged as something of an expert in the field of animal welfare. Mrs Fitzgerald's current investigation aims at the heart of the supply of performing dogs and other animals – to Mrs Latimer. Mrs Fitzgerald is not the sort to arm herself with a pair of dungarees and a pitchfork to monitor the daily care and feed of the animals. Reports from America suggest that Doris Day has been visiting the new homes of dogs adopted from their local pound. She rakes her film star fingers through the animals' fur looking for fleas, and she goes into the owners' kitchens to check on the freshness of the water in their drinking bowls, although whether she tests this by actually drinking the water is not clear.

Mrs Fitzgerald does not operate like this. In the first instance, she asks the questions and tracks down the answers from her office and her home in Brixton, visiting the suspects' premises in person only when she needs to collect forensic evidence.

Mrs Fitzgerald has checked Venetia Latimer's animal balance sheet: elephants in, elephants out. 'Where has she hidden that elephant?' Mrs Fitzgerald asks, over and over again. There is one elephant that has not been accounted for.

Mrs Fitzgerald looks into the accounts and assesses the quality and supply of feed, the integrity of the relationship with the supplier, the regularity and nature of medical care, the turnover of staff and the provision of training. She inquires into the pressures created by client expectations; she collects anecdotal evidence from past and current employees. Mrs Fitzgerald is a professional investigator, with all the resources of her profession at her fingertips. Mrs Latimer is a professional animal trainer, treading the fine line between discipline and cruelty. As Mary Chipperfield once famously remarked of an elephant in her care, 'I'm not beating it, I'm encouraging it with a stick.' If Mrs Latimer crosses the fine line, Mrs Fitzgerald will find out. Mrs Fitzgerald cares very much about animals.

In Paradise, Sylvia is dreaming about the circus again. On special nights like this, images of the twentieth century's greatest and most dazzling aerialistes and high-wire performers thread through Sylvia's dreams. Sometimes they appear as they were in their heyday, strong men and women in their sparkly costumes performing one more time for her benefit. More often than not Sylvia sees them as the active elderly people they grew into before departing the temporal world for their final destination.

They come into the dream all together, grey-haired and limber, dressed gracefully in loose-fitting jersey and cotton leisure wear. Their hands are linked and their arms extend from their sides, forming a vee with each other. They dance, forming a chain, pointing with the left foot, bending their knees and kicking up with the right heel, heads turned, smiling, hair flying all in the same direction with the motion of the dance. Then they come back again, pointing with the right foot, kicking with the left.

Sylvia tries to recognize them as they pass. There is Judith Gordon Innes who died aged eighty-seven. In the thirties she topped a human pyramid on a high wire as the only British member of the Great Wallendas. There is Joseph Hodgini who died aged one hundred and two. His wife Etta Davis is next to him. She had a high-wire and knife-throwing act with her twin Rita before marrying Joseph and joining him in his comedy riding act.

When he has been dancing in Sylvia's dreams in Paradise, Joseph Hodgini sometimes finds his way to where Venetia Latimer is sleeping in her house in West Sussex. He is Venetia's favourite animal trainer. She chose her son's name as a tribute to him. As a boy Joe Hodgini rode horses bareback in German and Russian circuses as Miss Daisy, a female impersonator. In the fifties he worked with a dog troupe, the first man ever successfully to train dachshunds for the circus. Venetia Latimer's dreams are male-dominated, as the profession of animal training tended to be in those earlier years. It is not something that troubles Venetia, she has never yearned for female companionship. She would rather enjoy the company of Jack Smith, unrivalled trainer of big cats and bears, the man who prepared the lions for their role in the film *Quo Vadis*, as he trades circus gossip with Poodles Hanneford who, in an earlier era, delighted audiences with his comedy riding turns.

Venetia Latimer never sees herself in these dreams but it is enough that her heroes are there, chatting as informally amongst themselves as if they were guests being treated to a fork supper at her house in Sussex.

In Brixton, every one of the twelve hundred dancing bears in captivity in India parades through Mrs Fitzgerald's crowded, horrible dream. Helplessly, she watches them twisting their tortured bodies to earn a few rupees for their owners. Even in her dream she knows she's too far away to help them slip the chains attached to their nostrils by rings sunk into the tender parts of their flesh.

From Spain, herds of stampeding bulls thunder into Mrs Fitzgerald's dream, blood spraying from the puncture wounds in their slippery, sweating hides where they have been speared and stabbed deep into the muscle underneath. Flecks of foam fly from between their bared teeth. The doses of strychnine they have been given have dulled the pain, not the fury. Their eyes are wild. As Mrs Fitzgerald watches, they start to tumble, front legs buckling first, then the hind legs, animal piling on top of animal as they fall.

She turns, restlessly, half awakes, then falls back to sleep. There is no respite. North America's diving mules rain from the skies in her dream. Tempted by as little reward as a carrot, they risk death or serious injury by jumping from high platforms into shallow pools below, urged on by the showmen who make money from their recklessness. Mrs Fitzgerald watches them come down, splayed hoofs splashing as they hit the water, jaunty straw hats floating away as they scramble to the edge of the pool, ready to jump again for another meagre reward.

When she wakes next morning, Mrs Fitzgerald sets to work early, redoubling her efforts to help the suffering creatures within her circle of influence on mainland Britain.

7

The Zebra

A group of her employees are putting the dogs through their paces in a muddy field near Mrs Latimer's house. They jump extravagantly through hoops. Repetition makes perfect. The trainers are as enthusiastic as the dogs. It's sometimes difficult to tell who enjoys the games more – the men or the animals. Everyone in the field is terribly pleased with the results.

A lad with a zebra stands and watches the dogs for a while. As the training session reaches its 'towering inferno' finale, he notices he's desperate for a pee. The walk back to the lavatory in the house is a long one and he has nowhere to park the zebra once he gets there. He walks over to the edge of the field, where the dogs have been taught to leave their mess, and fishes inside his combat trousers. In neat and tidy Amsterdam the phenomenon of 'wild pissing' is a nationally acknowledged problem, the streets flowing with smelly urine as the local men relieve themselves in public after a night on the beer. The lad smiles as he remembers his cousin's stag night in that city. A drop of virgin's water on the straw here in Sussex won't hurt.

The zebra keeper and some of the other young men who work at Mrs Latimer's have discovered that one of the medicines she feeds to the animals works well as a recreational drug. It's better than E. And it's free. This discovery has had a profound effect on their behaviour. They are all agreed on the need to keep the old lady sweet so she doesn't check up on them and start putting the stuff under lock and key. No one has stepped out of line, or given her any lip or even so much as turned up late for work since they started experimenting with the animals' drugs. It is vital to ensure the supply doesn't dry up until they can find out what's in it and work out a way to get cheap copies made by the people who run the underground drugs factories, in Amsterdam or north London. In the meantime the zebra keeper and his friends have been stockpiling for the party next week. They are all really looking forward to it. It's going to be pretty crazy.

The young zebra keeper privately celebrates being able to hold his cock in a field and relieve himself without having to flash his arse to the world — one of the many advantages of being a man — by trying to spray as wide an area of the straw as possible as he pees.

8

Jeremy

Harvey keeps his mobile phone switched on while he waits for some friends in Old Compton Street in Soho. Known locally as Queer Street, it is a flourishing centre for coffee bars, kitsch household items and minimalist restaurants serving light lunches. A cursory visit to the area suggests gay men's lives revolve around ornaments and cappuccino. Perhaps they do.

'Harvey?'

'Jane? You sound echoey.'

'I'm upside down over the kitchen sink, Harvey, dying my hair. I think I've left the bleach on too long. My scalp has gone red and it's burning like a bastard.'

'Get the hairdryer on and come and meet me, you silly mare.'

Jane drives round and round Golden Square in Soho before she finds a parking space. She gets out and leans against the locked car door, scrabbling to retrieve her mobile phone from her handbag before it stops ringing. It stops, just as her hand closes on it.

A young man with blond hair appears and stands very close to her, one hand on the warm bonnet of her car. 'The birds in the hedgerows are singing out of tune. They mimic the sounds of mobile phones and car alarms. They can't hear properly because of the volume of traffic. It makes it difficult for them to mark their territory and find a mate. Did you know you were stopping the birds from singing with your car and your mobile phone?

'No.'

'Why don't you do something about it?'

He is powerfully built, handsome and passionate about birdsong. The dress he is wearing shows off his thighs and the muscles in his arms, like a Roman centurion's costume in a Hollywood epic. He smells of fresh sweat and Nivea. Jane contemplates taking a break from her relationship with Philippe Noir. Philippe shaves his head and wears black jeans and white T-shirts. He doesn't love her and Jane doesn't love him. She hasn't looked for love from a man since being betrayed by her first boyfriend, also a journalist. He was disfigured when he crashed the blue Ferrari he was driving on Hong Kong's treacherous South Bay road, while engaged in a sex act with an heiress.

'I could do something. What do you want me to do? Do you want publicity?' She watches him think about what she's said. 'I could get it for you, if that's what you want. I'm a journalist.'

'We're going to turn back time. We're going to hold London to ransom until the capital turns back the traffic.'

Jane thinks, if I put my hand inside the dress where it is open at the neck, and touch my fingertips to his collar bone, would the contact make a faint squeaking noise like polishing glass, or would my fingers glide over the sweat where it shimmers on his damp skin? She says, 'That sounds very cryptic. Turning back time. Do you want a drink?'

Jeremy follows Jane Memory to a fashionable gay bar she knows in Soho, so that he can outline his plans for stopping the traffic to her before she joins Harvey for lunch. Gay men go to some trouble to establish bars, restaurants and cafés where they can meet in the West End without jostling at the bar against puking football fans every time they want to get a drink. Then young women start coming in, for much the same reason, and also so that they can drink dry white wine together and say 'What a waste' every time a gay man walks past. Then straight men start coming in so all the gay men leave and set up somewhere else. This cycle is one of the many burdens of fashionability borne by gay people.

'That's very visual,' says Jane, more than once, as Jeremy outlines his plan. Perhaps she will two-time Philippe rather than finish with him, so that he can help her pitch the idea for a forty-minute TV programme that follows Jeremy and his rabble as they prepare to stop the traffic.

The restaurant in Old Compton Street is crowded but Jane squeezes easily past the other diners to where Harvey is waiting at a window seat. She is wearing tight, shiny black trousers in manmade fibres that twitch across her fleshless buttocks when she walks, accentuating her cinched waist. She has very small buttocks, a masculine characteristic like many others in her emotional and physical repertoire. Jane Memory is masculine, but in a ball-breaking, sassy, ambitious way that is attractive to men. She's not mannish. She dyes her hair blonde and can talk at length about women's issues. Almost every single one of her close friends is homosexual.

'I'm trying to find a way of dealing with this fear of the unknown. I think I need to confront it first,' Harvey tells Jane over lunch.

'That's a good idea. There was something about confronting your fears in the Style section of *The Sunday Times* this week.'

'Who do I get advice from? A therapist? A Buddhist monk?'

'Darling, I'll give you the name of my spiritual healer.' Jane chews her spinach salad very thoroughly. A society woman once told her that the way to ensure none of it gets stuck in your teeth is to chew very energetically, moving your mouth when it is closed in such a way that your lips rub against your gums like windscreen wipers and sweep the spinach away.

'Really, you've got a spiritual healer? I didn't know you had any spirituality at all.'

'Well, its more of a networking thing, but I can get you in. He's very good, I think. His glasses are exactly the same shape as the Dalai Lama's, which gives him tremendous credibility and creates an atmosphere of trust and sharing at the meetings.'

'I don't think I want someone who's very good, after all. Someone told me once that if you need advice, you shouldn't necessarily ask a successful person. You learn more from failure.'

'That's a very good point. I did this fantastic feature about diets, once, with quite a lot of input from my friend Alvin who has to be very careful with his weight. If you want to know about diets, you should ask a fat person. They can evaluate every single kind of diet around – low fat, high carbohydrate, high protein, cabbage soup – you name it.'

'I think I'm looking for a broken person.'

'Broken people are terribly depressing. If I can find you someone living successfully without a name or identity, would that help?'

'I suppose so. Jane, why do you like getting involved in my life?'

'It's a nurturing thing, Harvs.'

Alison is reading to Phoebe. They are sitting on Alison's bed. Taron is in the garden smoking a cigarette, watching them through the open French windows. Phoebe's eyes are fixed on Alison's face, watching her mouth move as she reads the words in the picture book.

'"The lion is floating down the river on a raft." Why do you think he's doing that, Phoebe?'

'Is he looking for his friends?' asks Taron.

'Is he? Is that why he was building a raft?'

'Well, I think he was miserable all the time and he stopped going out so his friends gave up on him and ran away.'

'Really? I didn't get that at all. Anyway, the monkeys stayed around. They were the ones who helped him build the raft. Phoebe, come back.'

'I don't think much of this book. Can you read *Melisande* next time, about the princess whose hair grows and grows?'

'Do you think it's suitable?'

'Oh yes. It's my favourite story. Are you coming out tonight?'

'I can't leave Phoebe.'

'I could get you a babysitter.'

'Next time.'

9

The White Van

Roy has explored and mapped Paradise, from the horseshoe seashore as far as the sign on the fence. He has cleared a small area near Sylvia's vegetable patch and built a scale model of her house using pebbles, shingle and driftwood. It's a task he started merely to pass the time but the accuracy of its execution has since become important to him.

Roy is a practical man and he's used to being busy. He was in charge of the maintenance of the buildings at Mrs Latimer's. He carried business cards with 'Facilities Manager' printed on it but he thought of himself as a handyman. Everywhere he went, he carried with him a battery-operated reversible screwdriver, a tape measure, a pen and a walkie-talkie. It was second nature to him to detach the radio from his belt every fifteen or twenty minutes, bring it up to his mouth, depress the switch and issue orders or ask questions of his staff over the air.

It takes some adjustment not to stop where he is standing and expect to connect to Sylvia to ask an important question, 'Why is there a fence in Paradise? Over,' pressing the receiver to his ear to try to discern the reply over the hiss and crackle. There are no walkie-talkies in Heaven. By the time he has walked all the way back to where Sylvia is working, the importance of the question usually diminishes to the point where he seldom asks her anything except whether she would like a cup of tea.

Walking back to the house one day, counting the paces from the furthest edge of the shore, Roy sees a white van speeding along the path away from the house. He stops still in astonishment at the first sight of an outsider in Paradise. Then he breaks into a run, waving. Standing still and waving is fairly straightforward but running and waving is more difficult, the waving slows him down. The dust thrown up around the disappearing white van disguises the wheels, giving it an other-worldly appearance, as if it is being transported everywhere on a cloud.

The van disappears, unheeding his stumbling, waving attempts to communicate with it. Roy is frightened and excited by the sight of the van, wondering what it portends. Perhaps it has been dropping off another of Sylvia's animal friends, newly demised and recently arrived from Earth. Perhaps it was collecting something. Roy decides to rush back to the house but then to say nothing, giving Sylvia the opportunity to explain in her own time, in case it is something sensitive.

She's sitting in the kitchen eating chocolate, daydreaming. The suspense is too much for Roy. 'I saw the van.'

'Yes. Deliveries.' When Sylvia eats chocolate she sucks each piece until it dissolves, rather than chewing it. Apparently it is not so fattening if you eat it that way.

'Delivering what?' Is Sheila here? Another elephant? His friend Brian Donald? A whole host of performing dogs?

'Delivering provisions. We were running out of things to eat, Roy.' She gets up very slowly from the kitchen table and switches on the kettle. 'And some paperwork I've been expecting.' She waves a brown envelope. 'Do you want a cup of tea?'

Roy is shocked and frightened by the emotions stirred by the possibility of the death of his friends and loved ones. Death is usually associated with loss but in this case it would involve a gain of some kind. In fact he'd be gaining more than he could cope with, if faced with the arrival of Brian Donald or Sheila or Sylvia's animal friends. But he'd like to see Sheila again. The thought makes his head spin. What would happen if Heaven and Earth met somehow?

Roy thinks about Sheila, so far away and impossible to reach. What is Sheila doing now? Is she weeping and helpless with grief, or is she coping as always, briskly getting on with things, organizing volunteers for the next hospital fundraising day?

Roy walks outside to his scale model of Paradise, removing a few of the faded blossoms and leaves that have blown onto it from Sylvia's flower beds, adjusting the angle of the twig fence, raking the earth with his hands. Then he walks off to the seashore, carefully pacing the distance.

10

Convenience

Sheila goes to the newsagent in Brixton Hill to buy a one-day Travelcard. The people who own the shop stand a foot higher than their customers on a platform behind the counter, smiling with infinite good humour. Theirs is the only local convenience store for a radius of two miles in which the people serving in the shop are prepared to engage in eye contact with the customers during any transaction. In every other shop, the young men who work there talk incessantly on mobile phones, punching the price of the shopping into the till with a very off-hand manner, as if the work is beneath them, which it may very well be, as they all drive expensive jeeps which they park outside and watch jealously through the windows.

Sheila takes a bus from outside the newsagent's to Clapham Junction and then takes a train on the West Sussex line to Mrs Latimer's house, as Roy used to do on the days when he worked there, cheating one of the disadvantages of living in London by making a twenty-five-minute journey against the commuter traffic.

Venetia Latimer, wary but sympathetic, receives her missing employee's wife with kindness and a cup of tea in the kitchen. She has had a little while to prepare for the meeting as Sheila's worried face showed up on the closed circuit TV system when she first entered the land surrounding the estate and it tracked her progress until she reached the kitchen, at the heart of Mrs Latimer's empire.

'I think he's alive,' Sheila tells Mrs Latimer. 'But I don't understand why he hasn't found his way back. If he were free, he'd find his way back home to me.'

Mrs Latimer understands. Sheila is talking about love. Mrs Latimer sympathizes enormously but there is nothing she can say to make Sheila feel better. There is never anything anyone can say in these circumstances. Everyone is unreachable in their own private hell. Perhaps Roy has run away and left Sheila. She'll come to terms with it in her own way in the end.

'I was wondering whether you could shed any light on his disappearance, Mrs Latimer.'

'I'm sorry?' Mrs Latimer is jarred out of her reverie on the pain of abandonment.

'Is there any reason, any business reason, why someone should keep Roy from coming home?'

Mrs Latimer stares, astonished. 'I'm sorry?'

'You have a very successful business empire, Mrs Latimer. Roy was a part of it. A small part of it. I know he worked here for less than a year but even so, I wondered if there was anyone who could have kidnapped him.'

'I'm sorry? I thought he, um, blew away.'

'He may have fallen into the hands of your enemies. I wondered if they would try to obtain your secrets from him. The training techniques for the performing dogs, for example.'

'But, my dear, why would they have waited until he, er, blew away to obtain this information from him? It doesn't make sense.' Mrs Latimer watches as Sheila's face collapses in pain. 'I'm sorry, I wish I could help you.'

'It's OK, I'm not working alone. I've hired a private detective to help me. She was very helpful and very supportive. "Only believe."'

'What?'

'That's what Mrs Fitzgerald said to me: "You'll find him. Only believe."'

'Only believe? Well, then, there is something I can do. I'll pay the detective's fees. As Roy worked for me, it's the least I can do. You can handle all the contact, I don't need to be involved at all. Just send me the invoices for the next three months and a copy of the reports she makes and I'll pay all reasonable expenses. If we haven't found Roy in three months then perhaps we should talk again. But we will, Sheila. Love will find a way. He'll be back with you in no time and we'll all be laughing about it at the Christmas party. Just some silly misunderstanding.'

Sheila's visit has put Mrs Latimer in a thoughtful mood. A little while after Sheila has gone she takes her credit card from her purse and telephones *The Times* newspaper. She asks the sales assistant at the other end of the telephone to place an advertisement on her behalf in the personal column two days later, on the anniversary of the death of the great Poodles Hanneford: 'It doesn't matter about the money. Please come back. V.'

'Is that it?' asks the assistant.

'It's enough,' says Venetia.

She walks into her study and opens a drawer in her desk. She takes out a faded report into the care of performing animals entitled 'Unkindness Kills'. The report deals with animals trained for film, television and circuses and those kept in zoos. It argues that teaching animals to perform is unethical. The author cites proven instances of cruelty by trainers and keepers. It lists the names of horses killed in steeplechases. Mrs Latimer flips it over and re-reads the familiar summary: 'If every person who reads this report refuses to approve of performing animals, withdraws their support, refuses to participate even as a spectator, this will wither the industry. There is no need to campaign or protest. Just walk away. The industry cannot survive without an audience. Only believe.' And then the initials at the bottom, 'E.F.'

Harvey is wiggling his hips to the tunes from Jane's *Live at Pride* CD as he inspects her fridge for something that isn't low fat to pick at over coffee.

'Harvey,' Jane growls as his hand falls on a stale doughnut, 'stop mincing around and coin a clever phrase for me that I can slip into this style piece I'm doing for *The Sunday Times*.'

'What's it about?'

'It's about how you can fit a beauty routine into your busy day as a housewife and mother. You just make face masks out of the kids' food.'

'Messy Mums?'

'Nah, too negative.'

'Stale doughnut?'

'Hmm, doesn't really make sense. Stale Doughnut. Messy Mum. Doughnut Mum. It still all sounds vaguely insulting. And it's not exactly Generation X or the Beat Generation.'

'Jane, honey, what are you talking about? I was asking if you wanted to share a piece of this doughnut with me. Still, if you're looking for a metaphor in your article, how about Doughnut Generation? Does that sound better? Sugary and yummy-looking on the outside, an empty space on the inside.'

'Harvey, you've cracked it. That's absolutely great. It's too good to restrict it to an article about mango face packs. I'll develop it and pitch it somewhere. Jane Memory writes wittily and pithily about the Doughnut Generation. Jane points out that we all look delicious but we are empty inside. Men purr, women purr, the standard of the literary style piece is raised to new heights, editors pay vast amounts of money. Stop pirouetting, Harvey.'

'I wasn't pirouetting.'

'There's a tea towel over there if you need to wipe the sugar off your trousers. I need to raise my profile in print journalism, and I'd like to get into TV.' It is six months since Jane Memory gave her cold heart to TV docu-soap director Philippe Noir but so far he has failed to respond with a job offer. It is a sore point. 'I'm really proud of what I've achieved in journalism but I want to go further. I'm terrified I'm not going to get the breaks.'

'Terrified? What do you fear most in the world, Jane?'

'Obscurity. At least it's easier to fix than a fear of the unknown.'

Harvey watches Jane scratching her coccyx with the blunt end of a ballpoint pen through her trousers. 'Jane, what colour is "oyster", would you say?'

'Red, orange, yellow . . . gained battle in vain . . . green, blue, indigo, violet. It isn't a colour at all.'

'When I was a student at art school I worked weekends in the carpet department of a large furniture store. I handled telephone complaints. "They've delivered the wrong colour carpet," customers would say. "I ordered oyster but this is too dark, it doesn't look oyster-coloured at all. This is more of a gun-metal grey." Or dove grey or slate grey. "But that is the carpet you chose from the sample you saw in the showroom," I would tell them. "Oyster is just a label we use." It happened all the time. Doesn't that surprise you? People expected the carpet to match the colour that the name painted in their head rather than the sample they'd chosen with their own eyes. They would actually call me up and argue about the name we gave to the colour.'

'It doesn't surprise me at all, Harvs, people will do anything to get a discount.'

Mrs Fitzgerald sits on the top deck of a 159 bus as it waits at traffic lights at the square roundabout formed by Parliament Square in Westminster. The bus is in one of the three lanes of traffic that is nearest to the Houses of Parliament. Mrs Fitzgerald looks down and to her right, where a policeman in a box with a pointed roof guards the entrance to the House of Commons car park.

Mrs Fitzgerald looks at the statue of the crusader king Richard I, Coeur de Lion, riding his horse in front of the Houses of Parliament, his rapier sword raised in his right hand. He never did much for this country, plundering the gold reserves to pay for his wars against the Muslims (or Infidels, as they were known then). But he cut a very dashing figure, and his aggressive foreign policy did no harm to his popularity at home.

A young man on the path catches Mrs Fitzgerald's eye as the bus moves off slowly to the left. He is swinging his arms, taking long strides. The hem of his summer cotton dress brushes his knees as he walks. Mrs Fitzgerald turns completely round in her seat, rising up a little to catch a further sight of him but he has disappeared. If he was even there in the first place. She stares back through the rear window of the bus at Big Ben for a while, its façade familiar and reassuring, as the bus passes by Downing Street and Horse Guards Parade on its way up Whitehall towards Trafalgar Square.

Big Ben is the name popularly given to the Gothic clock tower which stands 316 feet high on the north side of the Houses of Parliament, although it is properly the name of the biggest bell in the tower that chimes the Westminster chimes on the hour, every hour. The bell weighs $13\frac{1}{2}$ tons, cast in the Whitechapel Bell Foundry in 1858. Some sources say the bell was named after Sir Benjamin Hall who commissioned the building. Others, perhaps given its East End provenance, suggest the bell was named after boxing champion Big Ben Caul who went sixty rounds unbeaten.

Each of the four clock faces is $22\frac{1}{2}$ feet in diameter. The individual numerals are nearly 2 feet tall. The minute hands are 14 feet long. Each one will have traced an arc of more than 5 feet in the five minutes since Mrs Fitzgerald first saw Jeremy making his way towards the clock tower.

Venetia Latimer looks at the kitchen clock. Eleven-thirty p.m. She is worried about her husband. She has left him sitting in the next room, his elbows propped on the worn arms of his chair, his head held in his hands as if it has grown too heavy to be supported by his neck. What use are you? she thinks, not unkindly. He's worrying about his job, she can tell. His new boss is giving him a hard time.

There is no point any longer in being a businessman, a technician or a tradesman, if you are a man. Women can learn the skills and perform those jobs as well as any man, or better, apparently, in the case of her husband's new boss.

A man who joins a large company is provided with a pension plan, a swipe card to get in through the front door and a bushel so he can hide his light under it. It certainly isn't the kind of work Mrs Latimer would have chosen for her son. She would rather he was a showman – a circus performer or an actor. Venetia suspects that men will be valued in the future only so long as they are frivolous; exotically and notably different from women.

Venetia puts a cup of milk in a large pan and boils it very rapidly, cutting the flame under it as it swells suddenly to twice its volume. She whisks two heaped teaspoons of Cadbury's milk chocolate and a tablespoon of brandy into the frothy milk, moves the pan, re-lights the flame and holds a marshmallow over the flame on the end of a fork until it forms a blistered skin on the point of bursting and sputtering its liquefied centre. She stirs the marshmallow into the hot chocolate, pours it into his favourite cup, sprinkles some finely chopped almonds on the top and walks next door to where her husband still sits. The brandy has curdled the milk, slightly.

He looks so gloomy that she can't think of any words that will make him feel better. She takes his hand, so he will draw comfort from her presence. At times like these a very small part of Venetia is sorry she disapproves of his career in the City so strongly because it makes it so difficult to discuss things with him. She has a horror of mentioning his unhappiness in case he starts talking about business issues and bores her.

'Stephen, I've brought you a cup of hot chocolate.' Venetia hopes the drink will cheer him up. She's really very fond of him. She has something she needs to ask him.

'Stephen, how would I go about getting a private detective's licence revoked?'

'A licence? I don't know how it works. If it's anything like a trading licence in the City then exposing the detective for something like embezzlement or drug dealing would do it. Can you try to turn up any kind of irregularity in his behaviour or in his business accounts? That would probably get a suspension, at least. Shall I tell you how it works in the City?'

'No. That's quite enough. You've been very helpful. Thank you.'

11

Colours

Roy watches Sylvia harvesting winter firewood from yesterday's pruning in the garden. Wearing gloves, she rubs one hand up and down the soft shoots on the branches to remove the leaves. She takes the very ends of the slimmest branches in her two hands and bends them until they break, the muscles tensing in her upper arms and her back under her tight pink T-shirt. Other, thicker branches are trimmed and cut to length with secateurs. Sylvia parcels them up using garden twine and places them lengthwise in a shoebox shaped woven basket with a handle to take them to the wood store, which is actually a garden shed. The leaves and twigs that she can't use for firewood in the kitchen and the living room are sorted into piles, the leaves going on to a compost heap and the twigs carried to a brazier in the back of the garden to be burned with the household rubbish.

There is something different about the orchard at the bottom of Sylvia's garden this morning. Roy looks very carefully at it through the foliage of the rose bushes that frame the kitchen window. Something has changed. Spring is coming but it's not that. He studies the view from the window. Soft shoots and hard buds are appearing on the flowers and trees, red and green among the grey. Clematis has wound itself through the rose branches, teardrop flower buds poking out at the top like little green vipers standing on their tails above a nest of prickles.

Roy looks through the sunlit space among the roses to where the sunlight reaches the apple trees. He watches two of the trees pick themselves up and move away, slowly. He looks again and sees they are Sorrel the elephant's legs moving, not the apple trees. Roy loses sight of her among the trees, then catches the movement again as she walks down to the beach. He feels lonely, watching her unobserved.

Ella Fitzgerald is potting up the geranium cuttings that have over-wintered on the window ledge in her spare bedroom. The leaves are variegated; soft green with thin maroon lines traced in them. She touches the leaves and the contact intensifies the distinctive, spicy smell in the air. The flowers, when they come, will be shocking salmon pink and pepper red.

Ella thinks about her husband, long since dead, who suffered from colour blindness. Men are more prone to the condition than women. Four per cent of men suffer from colour blindness, compared to one per cent of women. She pauses for a moment in sympathy for those who will never enjoy the garish clash of geranium colours when the flowers start to appear on the plants. How can such vibrant, different colours be indistinguishable? Her husband never liked to discuss it. He couldn't explain whether he perceived the colours as a muddy mixture or whether he saw both red and green as some exotic extra colour that she didn't have access to through normal vision. He only said that he couldn't see the difference between them.

There is a very rare colour blindness in which everything appears as a shade of grey, like a black and white photograph, or a television advertisement for an expensive perfume. Also very rare is blue blindness, in which sufferers are unable to detect the colour blue. More common is green blindness, in which bright green is confused with dark red, and red blindness, in which dark green is confused with light red. Mrs Fitzgerald's husband, whose disability would have disbarred him from taking a job as a signalman on the railways or a pilot on an aircraft, had chosen a career in the law and made a great success of it. Mrs Fitzgerald sighs a very tiny sigh, thinking about her lost husband.

She turns to the pots. She's using a compost that doesn't deplete the natural peat resources, emulating Geoff Hamilton, who until his death a few years ago was a stalwart in her life with his sensible advice on *Gardener's World* on Friday evening television. Mrs Fitzgerald sighs again. She sometimes feels she goes on and on through life, carrying its burdens, as men fall away. The earthy smell of the compost connects her to deep thoughts. She brushes away the dirt that clings to her fingers up to the first joints where she has plunged them into the pots and she walks away from the plants.

In the kitchen, her hands scrubbed and smelling of rose soap, Mrs Fitzgerald takes up one of the biographies she has been reading lately. She is conducting private research into the behaviour of people whose start in life is outwardly normal but who later descend into madness. She reads about troubled comedians, shamed politicians, drink- and drug-addicted foot- ballers, power crazy businessmen. What is it that connects them? Are there any external contributory factors? She deduces the link in one of those flashes when the staringly obvious hits for the first time. Every single one of the people in the books she has been reading has been damaged by notoriety. To ensure she learns from their mistakes, Mrs Fitzgerald vows to avoid notoriety at all costs. She pours a cup of very strong black coffee and opens a packet of Langue De Chat biscuits to celebrate her decision.

'There's so much colour in my life,' Alison tells Taron as the second shot of tequila goes down. 'Do you remember the first time you came here and everything in the house was white? The walls, the bed linen, the furniture? Now there are primary colours in every corner; toy trucks and postboxes and ABC books.'

'Hey, keep up. That uptight white stuff was so early-nineties-single-woman. Things have moved on. You only had colour in your garden when I met you. It was symptomatic of your empty life. Now you're enriched and fulfilled and there's colour everywhere. I think we should celebrate that.'

They lick the backs of their hands, sprinkle some salt, lick it, pour the tequila, pour the champagne, swirl, swirl, cover the glass, bang, bang, bang, drink the liquid, suck the lime.

'Aren't Tequila Slammers a bit of an eighties drink?'

'Alison, some things are evergreen. What's it really like, then, bringing up the baby?

'Say you buy a Volkswagen Golf.'

'Yes?'

'You don't expect to come home and find it's extruded into a Volvo and you can't park it anywhere.'

'That would take a bit of getting used to.'

'Exactly.'

Alison composes a poem to send to Jeff.

> Colours
> Colours are wrapping me up in my living room
> Coming in from the garden
> Climbing the walls of the nursery
> Red trucks in the corners
> Yellow plastic crockery in the sink
> Green elephants in my bed
> Taron says it's a sign of my coming of age

But I've never believed
A single thing
She's said.

'You will be sent to poet hell on Judgement Day to suffer eternal punishment with Murray Lachlan Young,' Taron tells her, and signals the end of the night by lighting up the last cigarette in the packet.

12

Cherry Lip Gloss

The psychic postman brings a small package in a brown Jiffy bag for Alison the next morning. It contains a present of cherry lip gloss from Jeff.

'My sister-in-law had a baby last year. She stopped going out or taking an interest in herself. A visit to the hairdresser, a touch of lipstick, you'd be surprised how much better she felt when she made a bit of an effort with her appearance.'

A handwritten poem falls from the package as Alison opens it.

Cherry Lip Gloss
Cloudy colour
Sticky flavour
Slicks your lips

Temporary
It slips away
With the first lick

Alison goes into the kitchen to make some lunch. A *Sunday Times* colour supplement feature on economical natural beauty techniques comes to mind. Standing at the hob, stir-frying things to a pulp in a wok, she slicks her fingers with olive oil and runs them through her hair and traces them over her dry lips. She mashes an avocado, spoons half the quantity into Phoebe's mouth and smears the rest on her face. The postman is probably right. She needs to get out more.

13

Truly, Madly, Deeply

Sheila Travers had no idea how much she depended on Roy until she lost him. She was always the strong one, the one who spoke for both of them and made all the trivial decisions about their daily lives. He didn't seem to care about anything much except her, which was one of the reasons she liked him. He fixed his brown eyes on her and watched her wherever she went in the house, like a faithful hound. Now that he has gone, her world is crumbling and she spends hours scouring the press and the TV and radio for clues to his disappearance.

The police haven't found his body. The only explanation for his continued absence that Sheila can come up with is that Roy is alive but he isn't free. Friends seem to feel that another explanation is much more likely.

'A woman? Why would a woman want to keep Roy from coming home?' Sheila asks them, puzzled. It's considered old-fashioned to differentiate between the genders but surely people still concede that men are more likely than women to commit crimes against the person?

'Are you saying he has simply been plucked from the air?' counter her friends, despairing.

Sheila, queuing in the newsagents to buy a newspaper, fire

lighters, bin liners and a packet of Twiglets, looks at the range of magazines with their incredible stories to tell. She has some understanding of the way that journalists work, having watched a docu-soap on the subject last year. Each one of the stories will have been carefully verified by the editor before going to print.

'My mother stole my boyfriend.' 'I spent the night in a spaceship.' *Are you saying he has simply been plucked from the air?* The mist clears. Sheila, wearing her favourite earrings, receives another message. Roy has been taken away. He hasn't come home because he can't get back. He is being studied or held to ransom by aliens.

When Sheila telephones the police, they are willing to consider a wider spectrum of possible explanations. 'An affair?' they suggest. 'Another woman? Another man? A mid-life crisis, a joke, a hoax, a fraud of some kind?'

Looking out at the sea from where he stands on the high-wire platform next to Sylvia's house, Roy wonders what would happen if he jumped from here, instead of trying to walk on the wire. Would it hurt? He cannot die, if he is dead already. If you die in Heaven, do you go to Hell? Do you drop to some other circle of Heaven that is less comfortable? Roy would rather stay here. He thinks about Sheila, as he often does, unreachable because he is dead and she is alive. If only there were some way of letting her know that he is all right. If only he could go back, like Alan Rickman in *Truly, Madly, Deeply*. Roy remembers walking Sheila home from the cinema after she'd been to see it with her sister, holding her as she sobbed. She said it was heartening the way someone with a big nose can get a starring role in a film and the woman was very convincing when she cried. It made her proud to be British. What was the name of the actress? Sylvia refuses to talk about her previous life but sometimes Roy slips in a reference to some cultural event to estimate how long ago she left Earth.

'Who was in *Truly, Madly, Deeply*?' Roy asks Sylvia, going to find her where she is kneeling in the vegetable garden, pulling up weeds. 'Julie something. Julie Walters? Julie Christie?'

'Juliet Stephenson,' she says, not looking round. So she was there somewhere, ten years ago or so, when he was walking home with Sheila. Would she have looked at him, if she'd walked past? He'd have looked at her with her bright hair and her pretty face. It is difficult to tell how she would feel about him under different circumstances because here he is one of a choice of one.

Maybe she was never alive. He likes to say to himself that Sylvia is an angel, although he doesn't feel that he is an angel. Has she undergone some sort of transformation that he has not yet completed, or do angels begin as angels? Was she in a holding place somewhere in the clouds, in some other Heaven where there is a giant video screen where she and all the other waiting angels could watch the latest releases? She hasn't been here for ever because she has told Roy that the land was overgrown and ugly when she first arrived.

'How old is that dog?'

Sylvia's elderly sheepdog totters by. It is black with a white patch on its face and white paws. One green eye, one blue. 'She's sixteen.'

'That's old.'

'Yes. She was nearly fourteen when she came here.'

The dog has continued to grow older even after it has died. This information is a bombshell for Roy. Horrible, horrible information. Will he continue to age while he's here? He thought he'd done well to stick at forty-two but he will grow older and older with no prospect of release, as there is on Earth.

14

The Dinner Party

Miss Lester, zipping across town on a very small moped, is vibrating with excited nervous energy. She has never, ever been so happy. The cause of this happiness is Ella Fitzgerald, who has accepted Miss Lester's business proposal to set up a dinner party dating agency, using her own offices as its headquarters.

Miss Lester had been feeling rather low since the failure of an affair. This coincided with her departure from a management position in the genetics industry, under circumstances which left her reluctant to seek alternative employment with anyone who might wish to take up references. However, the rehabilitating effects of Mrs Fitzgerald's trust and kindness have been remarkable. Miss Lester has thrown herself into the task of setting up the dating agency, compiling business plans, charts and projected returns on investment. She has equipped herself with an infrared pointer pen, of the kind that have been banned in schools and provincial nightclubs, and she has made lengthy presentations to Mrs Fitzgerald and all her associates.

For the very first round of dinners, Miss Lester has pulled in some favours, filling some of the spare places with people who are not genuine love-seekers, just to get the evening going with a swing.

Speeding through Soho's stationary traffic astride her moped that evening, like a winged emissary from the gods bringing happiness to London's single professionals, Miss Lester is struck by a pale face staring at her from the shadows as she draws to a stop at a set of traffic lights. A man in a dress steps out in front of her, as if daring her to drive through him when the lights change, his eyes holding hers for a few seconds through the visor of her crash helmet. The malevolence in the gaze unsettles Miss Lester even after the man crosses to the other side of the road, continuing his journey without looking back.

As she arrives at the restaurant, Miss Lester sees that things have already gone slightly awry, with people moving the place cards and spoiling the boy-girl, boy-girl symmetry of the seating arrangements.

Mrs Fitzgerald's associate Alison is sitting there with a scowl on her face. Alison's best friend Taron is sitting on her left. Her friend and neighbour, Harvey, is sitting opposite. To Alison's right is Hugo Fragrance, a stunningly handsome man who works in the City and can talk of nothing else.

Miss Lester, unaccustomed to wearing make-up, has selected a too-sticky lipstick that has already travelled over the edges of her mouth. She has the appearance of being made up of a series of interlocking triangles. Her face is an inverted isosceles triangle framed within the equilateral triangle of her hair. Her nose is a triangle. Even her clothes are triangular because she wears knee-length A-line skirts.

Miss Lester has chosen to set up a dating agency because her research has shown it will deliver a high return on her investment capital. Miss Lester is perfectly competent when it comes to pointing at a flip chart with an infrared pen and saying, 'Our vision is to be the best dating agency in Britain,' but she hasn't got much grasp of how to organise a successful dinner party. Nevertheless, she has already obtained, from one

Miss Lester *Miss Lester − side view*

of her guests, the phone number for renowned director Philippe Noir, with the aim of interesting him in filming a docu-soap about her company for Channel Four. One of the best things about being on TV is that she would hope to be able to repay Mrs Fitzgerald in some small way by ensuring the director gives her benefactor plenty of prime-time exposure.

Tonight, the dinner party conversation ranges between the jobs in the City held by the paying guests, what is happening in the news and the food being served. Taron and Alison aren't hungry because they have been doing drugs in the toilet. This gives them more opportunity to talk than the other guests, who are restricted to talking between mouthfuls. Unfortunately, their contribution to the conversation isn't grounded in any real understanding of the City, current affairs or indeed what the food tastes like tonight.

'Mmm, this pork in cider is terribly tender,' says one of the City chicks of her hearty and rustic main course. The red wine has brought a bloom of purple to her tongue and to the grainy deposit in the cracks at the corners of her mouth.

'Alison read in the paper about this man who drank a whole

flagon of cider while he was babysitting. The mother came home and found the baby's legs sticking out from under him where he'd fallen asleep on it on the sofa,' says Taron, deftly picking up the threads of the conversation to weave the subject of the food into current affairs.

'Did the baby survive?' asks the man to Taron's left, looking carefully at her magnificent bosoms as if the answer were to be found written across them in very small print.

'No, it was dead by the time the mother came home.'

Alison chooses this moment to sneak off and call Darren the babysitter at home. Darren has ginger hair and green nail varnish, supplied for the purpose for the evening by Taron; he was chosen for the unlikelihood of his being fazed by Alison's late return after her first night out in four months. The down side was his apparent astonishment at the concept of dialling 999 in an emergency, which had to be explained to him several times.

A couple of the City men move closer to Taron and stare at her. They lean forward, close enough to touch but not touching. The women at the other end of the table, having read in *Cosmo* that some men have difficulty in reading subtle body language, and unwilling to take the chance that Harvey is one of them, are crowding round him and each of them is holding on to a piece of him. One woman is reading his palm, another is kneading his thigh muscle. Another stands just behind him and squashes one bosom against the back of his head under cover of reading the dessert menu on the table.

All the women smoke between courses. 'It's supposed to be a mystery why successful and attractive men and women can't get it together and have to join dating agencies,' muses Alison, leaning over so Taron can hear. 'But on the evidence of the evening, it's obviously attributable to the fact that all the women smoke and all the men are complete knobs.'

'Except Harvey.'

'Except Harvey.' Harvey, catching his name, looks round and smiles. He's acting his part very well for the evening, handsome and hetero in charcoal grey, having removed all his jewellery for the occasion.

One of the women at the dinner table starts on a fairly innocuous topic of conversation that segues into how interesting and busy she is: 'I much prefer dogs to cats, don't you? Mind you, I have to make do with a cat because of my lifestyle. I'm out most nights and I have such a demanding job that I have to get into work very early to get through everything.'

'My mother breeds dogs,' says a quiet young man called Joey who has loops of springy hair piled on top of his head and very bright blue eyes. 'She trains them for adverts. She loves them. I think she loves them because she can control them.' It's his one opportunity to make an impression on the others round the table but he's blown it because they're already off on another topic, led by Taron. She's abandoned any pretence at discussing neutral topics that flow naturally from the conversation and is shouting out anything that comes into her head. Alison leads her away to the toilet to give the others a chance to shine.

From the washbasin she calls out to Taron, still in the cubicle, 'My hair's getting triangular.'

'Like Miss Lester.'

'Do you think that's my destiny? Will I slowly turn into Miss Lester as I get older?'

Taron emerges and meets Alison's eyes in the mirror. Without washing her hands, she reaches up and curls strands of Alison's hair round her fingers, as if she's trying to make ringlets. 'Cheer up, Alison,' she says, tugging the hair gently, still holding her eyes in the mirror.

In the taxi on the way back home to their loft apartment in

Clerkenwell, Joey Latimer and Hugo Fragrance have a debrief of the evening's events.

'Taron was great. She was a good laugh. The best thing about her, really, was—'

'Top quality drugs?'

'Yeah, well, she had some good stuff with her. The best thing about her was she's exactly the kind of girl my mother would like.'

'She hardly said one word to you all night.'

'Well, I spoke to her when I left. I invited her to the party in a fortnight.'

'Your mum will be really relieved if you bring a sparky bird like that home with you, after all the money she's spent on signing us up for those dreadful dinners.'

'Do you reckon that lad Harvey was a poof?'

'Yep. It was written all over him.'

'Where've you been?' Harvey asks Alison, opening the door to their house in response to the scratching sound she's making near the lock with her key.

'To a club.'

'At your age?'

'I didn't like anyone at that dinner party except you and Taron. The club was much more my scene.'

'You probably gave the people on the door a heart attack. No one wears smart casual to a club except the drugs squad.'

'I had a halter neck under the jacket. Once I'd given my pound to the old bag to guard it in the cloakroom, I was transformed into a party princess. The lighting kills the wrinkles and my eyes are gobstoppers under these lashes.'

'A princess? So, did you meet a handsome prince?'

'It's so easy to pick up a man in a club, isn't it? I'd forgotten.

As soon as I walked in the door, a stranger held out his lighter for me as I put my cigarette to my lips.'

'I thought you'd given up smoking.'

'Give me a break. After that dinner party? Anyway, I always smoke when I'm drunk.'

'OK, so what else?'

'Another man slipped his arm around my waist.'

'Very intimate.'

'Much too intimate, considering I was all bare skin and nipples in that halter top. He didn't say anything, just clung on to me and moved in time to the music.'

'Well, did you say anything to him?

'His eyes were vacant – he looked as if he was trying to remember something. I had a bottle of water in my hand, glowing like a luminous baton in the ultraviolet light. He took it from me three times for a drink and each time he forgot to unscrew the lid before putting it to his lips. I didn't say anything, I just wriggled out of his grasp. There was a girl with a smile that lit up her face as she danced. Her whole body revolved round her smile. I went up to her and said, "You've got a beautiful smile." She said, "You've got a beautiful body."'

'You have.'

'Well, you can't tire of hearing something like that. Every so often I'd sidle up to her again and say, "You've got a beautiful smile." I got the smile but that was it, she didn't mention my body again. Then at the end of the night a boy of around eighteen walked up to me as I was dancing and slipped his hand between my legs.'

'A rather novel kind of greeting.'

'"Weren't we at school together?" he asked. Maybe he thought I was a teacher. He had a sensuous, soft mouth, his hair was damp at the temples, his arms were slim, like a girl's.'

'And what?'

'And nothing. He recognised me because twenty minutes before he'd asked me for a cigarette so he could skin up in the bar upstairs. The music was too loud to try and explain so I disengaged myself from his hand and went to get my jacket.'

'So it was a good night?'

'I felt young and pretty, although the illusion is fading. I know my skin is mottled and my hair smells of fags.'

'No, darling. You are young and pretty and your hair is very fragrant, usually. You do look a bit blotchy, but that's probably an allergic reaction to the fabric on the seats from the taxi ride home.'

'My knees are aching. I think I may have overdone the dancing a bit, like an auntie at a wedding.'

'Shall I make you a cup of tea?'

'Yeah, sling some whisky in it, Harvey, to help me sleep.'

15

The Models

'I'm a model,' explains the young lady. 'Like my friend Felicity.'

Miss Lester has heard that once models have scrubbed all their makeup off their faces, they look very plain. It certainly seems to be the case with Felicity and her friends. They look plain even with a great many layers of make-up, but they are very keen to help out Miss Lester with her dinner dating agency, which has yet to get off the ground by attracting workable numbers of applicants to sign up for love.

Every Friday, Miss Lester has to find twelve people for each of five or six dinner parties across town. She needs to have a larger number of guests available than she currently has on her books so she can mix and match them, ensuring they don't dine with the same people every week. Fortunately, Miss Lester got talking to Felicity in the newsagent's on Brixton Hill one day. Felicity explained she was a model who would be prepared to make up the shortfall in the numbers at dinner in return for a free meal and wine and a bit of cash in her pocket.

Felicity has recommended a few of her friends who are prepared to help Miss Lester on the same terms. Miss Lester's latest recruit, Prudence, is rather a busty girl with very good skin. Miss Lester suspects that Felicity, Prudence and her friends are prostitutes. When she has finished interviewing Prudence, Miss Lester telephones Philippe Noir. She reaches his assistant, Harriet.

'I'm sorry, Miss Lester, prostitutes are commonplace on the television these days. Are any of them transsexuals?'

'Well, I don't think—'

'That's a relief, anyway. Philippe and I can hardly turn round in here for transsexual prostitutes seeking to make their fortune through the telly.'

'It isn't just the dating agency. A friend of mine runs a detective agency.'

'Really?'

'Yes, she's a real character.'

'Hold the line a moment.'

In her office next door to Miss Lester's, Mrs Fitzgerald takes a break from her scrutiny of Venetia Latimer's accounts for a meagre lunch of crispbread and celery. She wipes her hands carefully between each mouthful so she doesn't smear the borrowed copy of Paul Merson's *Rock Bottom* she has taken out from Brixton library to read in her lunch hour. *Diana, My True Story* is on top of a stack of books on the side table that she must return on her way home from the office. Mrs Fitzgerald shudders every time she catches sight of them because they make her think about the demons pursuing these people because of their fame.

'Miss Lester, are you still there? I'm sorry, we just can't do it. They've had customs officers and the RSPCA on the BBC, debt collectors on ITV, and the police on just about every channel, every day of the week. I don't think the market could bear another law enforcement type programme. Besides, Philippe's going global. He's not limiting himself to the UK at present. I could give you his girlfriend's number. She might be able to do something in print for you.'

16

Being Light

Harvey is lying on a thin mat in a warm room that smells subtly of feet. His quest for knowledge has brought him here, although he's not sure why. 'Everyone does yoga now, even Madonna,' explained Jane, booking him in.

'You are strong but you are not loose,' the yoga teacher tells him. Is that good? Harvey wonders. His head fills with questions all through the session. He is not comfortable with the dynamics of group teaching, he decides. He cannot tap into any sense of oneness. Behind him, someone breathes in ostentatiously through their nostrils, dragging mucus the entire length of their nasal passages and then making a triumphant 'Ha' sound on the out breath through the mouth. Everyone else in the group breathes quietly, including the teacher.

Harvey and the others in the group are clearing their minds of all thoughts as they relax at the end of the session. 'Imagine you are in a meadow on a summer's day,' the teacher tells them. Her voice is low and calming. Harvey can feel the sunshine. He can actually smell the grass.

A sudden tickle catches at his throat. Harvey cringes, every muscle in his body clenching with the effort of not allowing the tickle to erupt into a dry, explosive cough, shattering the peace for everyone. The teacher's measured voice continues. I am strong, thinks Harvey. I am not loose but I am strong. It feels like hay fever. Tears squeeze from his eyes and run down his face. His fists are balled. His toes curl in on themselves. His shoulders hunch up towards his ears. His diaphragm heaves but he keeps his lips pressed tightly together to prevent any sounds escaping and disturbing the others.

At last the other people get up from their mats and Harvey lurches out of the room to the water fountain in the corridor, tense, red-faced, apparently weeping.

Roy is sharpening the ends of sweet pea sticks so he can push them into the ground in a tent shape and train the sweet peas to climb them. He stops suddenly, in the middle of what he is doing, and stands right where he is without moving for a long while.

'I will never see Canada,' he says finally. It had always been a dream of his to visit Canada and meet up with a cousin who emigrated there in his twenties. They would go to Niagara Falls and swim in the Great Lakes. The itinerary had been the subject of jokey Christmas cards swapped each year between the two men, 'yes, every one of the Great Lakes', and it had been something he'd promised Sheila they would do one day in lieu of a glamorous honeymoon, which they hadn't been able to afford when they got married. Now he knows he will never go to Canada.

'Don't you feel free here, Roy?' Sylvia asks him. 'I don't have any worries at all. I feel as if one day I'll get so light I'll just spread my arms and rise up into the air a little way. I'd like to get so carefree that I feel I can fly again, the way I did when I was younger.'

'I feel quite heavy.'

'You haven't left your old life behind you yet. One day you'll feel so light and free you could run across the tightrope.'

'Like one of your elephants?'

'No, it's too late for that. I'll never know whether I could teach an elephant to walk across a tightrope, now.'

'Perhaps you could teach me.'

'Perhaps.'

Sylvia will never teach an elephant to walk the tightrope and Roy will never go to Canada. For Sylvia's sake, Roy makes an effort to feel light. This would show a commitment to Sylvia and to his new life in Heaven. Roy has never been able to tell people how he feels, only to try and show them. There were hundreds of ways he tried to show Sheila that he loved her, following her around the house and responding to every subtle change in her mood. He even fell in with Sheila's volunteering schemes, erecting bouncy castles on his days off with that idiot Brian Donald as a way of letting her know that he cared.

He hasn't talked to Sylvia about life in Heaven and what he makes of it or how happy he is here with her. He can only try to make himself light as a way of showing her. It seems to take a lot of practice, so perhaps it is fortunate that he has all eternity to perfect it. Sylvia, lethargic and plump, although in an attractive way, the way a plum is more attractive than a prune, can tumble effortlessly, over and over like a ball of dust blown by the wind. He has seen her run across the tightrope as if she were accustomed to running through the air.

17

Faecal Matter

Venetia Latimer is marking the end of the long life of a celebrated aerialist she never knew with a party at her house.

Mrs Latimer has the robust figure of a transvestite and has therefore never been airborne like her circus heroes. Her imagination was caught by the romance of the circus at an early age. She jumped up one morning and ran away from her nice girls' school and the prosaic future it was shaping for her and tried to join the circus. They brought her back and she ran away, they brought her back and she ran away, setting up a pattern she repeated at fourteen, fifteen, sixteen. It wrecked her chances of passing her exams but everyone pretended to believe it was due to a hormonal imbalance and let her re-sit them. She gave up running away but she never gave up the dream, she just worked out another way to get there.

Mrs Latimer lives the horsy, farmy life in West Sussex that has always been her destiny but she teaches the horses to jump through flaming hoops and she breeds performing dogs and other, more exotic, animals instead of pigs or sheep, supplying them to circuses and the film industry. Mrs Latimer has a virtual monopoly on the supply of performing animals, she has built an empire that is the envy of other animal trainers. She is a legend. She wields an immense power that comes from having an immense income and she can visit the circus whenever she likes without someone trying to fetch her back home.

Her only disappointment is her son Joey, who is firmly fixed on being something in the City like his father and his father before him. Mrs Latimer blames his public school education, which taught him lots of academic things but has rather restricted his outlook on life and made him shy with girls. Tonight, in one of a string of ongoing futile attempts to draw out and nurture the latent heterosexuality in her son's nature, Mrs Latimer has invited him to her party.

Mrs Latimer's wealth and status have bestowed power on her but the stronger power of the circus still makes her vulnerable. She's in love with the circus; hopelessly, profoundly, daydreamily besotted with it. Like many people in love, the love humbles her and makes her behave foolishly. In the exotic presence of terse, foreign, muscular circus artistes, Mrs Latimer makes a bundle of her articulacy, her business nous, her head for figures, her expensive private education, like a redundant bundle of clothes on a naturist holiday, and she lays it at their feet.

Her family wholeheartedly disapprove. There was a bit of silliness a couple of years ago when Mrs Latimer lost her head entirely over a circus girl who came to work with her. Mrs Latimer told all her business and professional secrets. She loved and admired and bundled herself up. She wrapped the glittering girl in her love, bandaging her in layers and layers of admiration and confidences and foolish love. Eventually the girl repaid her by stealing an elephant and a great deal of money and running away.

There are more than seventy candles alight in the house by the time Mrs Latimer's son arrives. The ones nearest the front door flicker slightly as he and his best friend Hugo Fragrance let themselves in quietly and join the party. Mrs Latimer's attitude to throwing parties is that she invites every single person she knows or has ever known without worrying about whether people will get on. The success is in the numbers rather than the mix.

Tonight, the guests are mixing well, ladling punch for each other from the Emphglott-sponsored crystal bowls awarded to champion dog breeders, and caressing the award-winning dogs sprawled on the sofas. There are several researchers from Emphglott who are trying to give the impression they are in TV, several TV researchers who are trying to give the impression they are producers, lots and lots of people from the village, high-flyers from the City, farm hands, dog hands, acrobats, trapeze artistes and elephant trainers, and Mrs Latimer's accountants who are having an affair and will slip away later and have sex. Almost everyone is hoping to get very drunk at Mrs Latimer's expense, except the people who have brought their own drugs.

Taron is talking to a young man wearing a dress. She can see the blond hairs under his arms, poking from above the sleeveless bodice, when he puts the bottle of beer to his mouth to drink. His short fingernails are painted a shade of baby pink that Miss Selfridge markets as 'Miss World'. His face is beautiful. He has a performer's swagger, as if he is used to being looked at and admired, but when he speaks he looks down a lot, as if he is really quite shy.

'Fifty per cent of trees planted in cities die in their first year,' Taron tells him. 'The parks departments are planting the wrong trees, they can't survive the conditions. They suffer horribly from the pollution. Even if they make it past the first year, their life expectancy is cut by one-fifth. I'm going to take some water containers out next week and give them a drink and try wiping some of the filth off their leaves.'

'I'm going to stop the traffic.' The young man smiles

suddenly, making dimples at the sides of his mouth. Taron, unsure whether this is an anti-pollution plan or a comment on his outfit, turns away to dip her cup into the bowl of punch.

On the temporary dance floor in the living room, very close to the speakers broadcasting a selection of Mrs Latimer's favourite tunes, the zebra keeper and his best friend are clinging together, cigarettes alight. Both have damp hair, grey faces, dilated pupils. They are grimacing, or possibly smiling, their expressions like teenagers on a scary fairground ride. Their teeth are chattering. 'Fucking hell,' whispers the zebra keeper, breaking away from his friend's embrace to find his bottle of poppers in the back pocket of his jeans.

The cloudy, moonless night conceals Mrs Fitzgerald, a little way removed from the house, wearing a very smart brown tweed skirt and pink Marigold gloves. She is crouching in a field collecting faecal samples and urine-soaked straw with Alison. Alison is dressed more casually but is taking the same sensible precautions in protecting her hands. Phoebe is with them in her stroller, wrapped against the chill of the spring evening, staring into the middle distance as children tend to do when they're with adults who are engaged in inexplicable tasks that don't involve them.

Mrs Fitzgerald is engrossed in the task of collecting the samples with a trowel and placing them in labelled plastic bags held open for the purpose by Alison. If a crowd of students from a local university were to walk by, one of them might comment, 'Ner, you're mad, you are,' but an engagement in the serious business of investigating is one of the occasions when Mrs Fitzgerald has no such doubts about her sanity.

'Harvey, I need your help.'

'That makes a nice change, Jane. Where are you?'

'I'm having a colonic.'

'Well, I suppose that is a change. You've never called me under such intimate circumstances before.'

'Yes I have. I can't interest any TV production companies in the story about Jeremy. I want to go ahead and make a short film anyway and use it as a show reel. I need you to do the camera work.'

'I made a film at art school, that doesn't make me Steven Spielberg.'

'Philippe can get me all the kit for free. I'll carry the fuzzy thing. It doesn't matter if it's in shot, I think it lends authenticity. Come on, Harvs, I'd do it for you.'

'You wouldn't.'

'Why are we friends, would you say? Is it because we both hate men?'

'I like men.'

'Oh yes. Is it because we both hate women?'

'I like women too. I like everyone and you hate everyone. It's an attraction of opposites.'

'Jeremy's got a sister who's run away from the world. She's living miles away. In the middle of nowhere, effectively. She's escaped her old identity. Do you see, Harvs? She's got no name and no sense of place. She's living in a void. If you do this teeny bit of filming I could get Jeremy to take us to meet her. Maybe she can be your guru. Just don't tell Jeremy that I can't get him on TV, I promised him some publicity.'

'Don't tell Jeremy? It sounds as if it's getting serious. Will you start wanting to take care of him?'

'No, taking care of someone is just a way of trying to control them.'

'You like to control people.'

'Yes, but I like to give them a list and say do this, do that. I don't want to arse about cooking some man a fried breakfast and ironing his shirts as a precursor to influencing all his decisions.'

'Well, why do it the hard way? You've certainly come up with a labour-saving strategy.'

'Did I tell you that I've been having sex with Jeremy?'

'Is it any good?'

'Yes, I really like him. Part of the attraction is that I don't really know what he's thinking, he's quite unpredictable. Do you remember when we bought those teen mags to pass the journey when we took the train to Cardiff?'

'Wasn't it Edinburgh?'

'Whatever. We completed all the quizzes for each other and ticked all the right boxes. It's great to know someone as well as I know you, don't get me wrong. But with Jeremy, I wouldn't know which boxes to tick.'

'Alison? It's Taron, I'm just back from Mrs Latimer's. Sorry, were you asleep? I wish you could have been at the party.'

'I was doing something. Anyway, I couldn't leave Phoebe. Never mind, how was it?'

'It was great. Do you remember going to parties as a child? There'd always be a party bag full of goodies to collect at the end of the night. I've never grown out of that, I hate to go home empty-handed from a party.'

'What do you mean? Did you bring a man home?'

'Not this time. There was no one there that I wanted. Mrs Latimer gave me a big parcel of food to take away, though, and two dozen candles.'

'Anything else happen?'

'I drank too much and got really trashed because I've given up drugs.'

'I didn't know you'd given up drugs.'

'Yeah, I just stopped getting high so I gave them up.'

'Maybe you need to try a different brand.'

'No. I feel about drugs the way I'd feel about an old love affair. It made sense at the time but I wouldn't want to go back and try again. I'm finding it quite difficult, though. If you don't do drugs you have these huge gaps in your life that you have to fill. Time goes really slowly and you have to be on the lookout for adventure the whole time. Drugs create a momentum of their own where you chase about finding a dealer, getting high, recovering, buying more drugs, getting high. It really fills up the spare moments. Now I've got so much quality time on my hands I don't know what to do with it all. And I get pissed all the time because I'm not used to drinking without taking drugs to temper the alcohol.'

'How long has this been going on?'

'Two weeks.'

'Two weeks? We were at Miss Lester's dinner party two weeks ago.'

'Well, ten days. Listen, Alison, drugs are just a fast track to some kind of excitement you recognize because you've experienced it before somewhere. It's like using a microwave instead of conventional cooking. Whether you're using drugs or not using them, you're still trying to get to the same place. All I have to do is remember how to get there the slow way.'

'Are you drunk now?'

'A bit. I feel pretty weird, actually. I think I'd feel toxic if I went anywhere near any more drugs. I've done so many over the years that one more little grain of anything might tip me over the edge. I may as well chew on pencil lead.'

'That won't do you any harm. They use graphite now. You'd have to lick tin soldiers in an antique shop. Was Joey at the party?'

'Yeah. He's really cute, he seems very fond of me.'

'And do you like him?'

'I've kind of taken him under my wing.'

'Under your wing? Where would that put him? In your armpit?'

'Alison. I thought you wanted me to go to the party so I could report back to you about Mrs Latimer. There's no point being rude or I won't tell you anything.'

'Well, did you find out anything about Mrs Latimer?'

'She loves me to death and there's something weird going on with her animals.'

'What kind of weird?'

'Have you ever seen a dog typing and smoking a pipe?'

'Like Ernest Hemingway?'

'They're like really bright undisciplined kids. They paint and chase rabbits and ride bicycles. There was a Doberman on the couch who looked as if it was reading a newspaper.'

'Is chasing rabbits necessarily a sign of weirdness in dogs?'

'No, but it is in children. I saw a programme on TV once about some posh kids who were allowed to do what they wanted at school and they chased a rabbit and killed it.'

'So what's happening with Joey? Are you going to start seeing him?'

'No, nothing like that. He's just going to help me out with a few of the projects I've got on at the moment. What about you, Alison? Why don't you get yourself a man?'

'Men are like cigarettes. I only want one when I'm drunk.'

18

Night-time

Watching the street outside their flat in vain for Roy's return, Sheila suddenly pulls up the sash window and leans out, looking up. She wouldn't be able to say why, if anyone had been there to ask her. Perhaps she was tired of breathing her own warm breath in the flat and she wanted to take in the cool, smoky London air for a change. Above her, hanging among the drifting clouds in the sky, is a very bright, ellipse-shaped light.

Sylvia likes to sleep naked in Paradise, drawing the pillows around her in her big bed as if to cushion herself against a potential fall while asleep. A family in England recently searched all night for their missing teenage daughter before realizing she had been safely tucked under the covers in bed the whole time. Roy would never make such a mistake with Sylvia; the curves of her body are accentuated under the patchwork counterpane in the places where she props pillows around her body. She slips one arm under the pillows at the head of the bed, hugging her face to them. She keeps one pillow at her back, cuddles another at her side under the crook of her arm, another under one bent knee, or between two bent knees. She is lying on her right side, watching the doorway.

When Roy comes into the room, smelling of toothpaste, she pushes all the pillows to the edges of the bed. The pillow that has been resting against her back is very warm when he lies his face lies against it. She makes a place for his left leg where one of the pillows touched inside her thighs and knees. Her body is hot, insulated against the night-time by the feathers that have been all around her. Even her feet are warm, when she slithers them across the sheets and puts them on Roy's feet. She keeps her eyes open but Roy can barely see them in the darkness. He puts his hand out to her face and touches it very softly, to be sure where her mouth is when he kisses her.

She puts her hand on his hips and presses him closer but he resists, arching his back slightly so that he can move his hand up her body and feel her bosom. He slips his left hand under the pillow at his head and finds Sylvia's right hand. He works his fingers into the palm of her hand so she will stop holding on to the pillowcase and he laces his fingers through hers.

He moves his right hand to her thighs, her bottom, the flesh above her hips. All the flesh has the same consistency as her breasts: firm, with a slight give when he presses his fingers into it. Oh my God, I'm fucking a giant breast, he thinks, just before he comes, in the moment that is like falling, when Heaven and Earth seem to fit together.

19

Usefulness

The zebra keeper is in his rented kitchen, lying on the ridged, prickly carpet near the fridge. The carpet is tough-wearing and of indeterminate colour, chosen by the landlord to withstand the enthusiasms of sloppy young men with an aversion to vacuuming. The zebra keeper is lying on the patch where the spilled food collects on its journey to and from the table.

The zebra keeper's name is James. He remembers this almost as soon as he wakes up. His left arm is slightly numb where he has been lying on it. His underpants have hitched themselves a little way into the cleft between his buttocks, which he now remedies with his good hand.

James's flatmate, Robert, another animal keeper and his best friend, walks bare-footed into the kitchen from his bedroom. He is also wearing the clothes he wore last night. He knocks James's head lightly as he opens the fridge door to find a beer. 'Man, that party was really kicking last night.'

James is sitting up, shaking his left hand vigorously and patting his discarded jacket with his right, trying to locate his cigarettes. 'Yeah,' he agrees. He begins to laugh. 'Every time I looked at the old lady, she seemed to be morphing into one of her animals.'

'She was necking the punch down.'

'So was everyone. I was tripping off my face but they were just tottering around, making small talk like nothing was happening.'

'The alcohol kills it. There wasn't really enough in the punch to do anything except put a sheen on things, although I chucked a bit on the chicken satay as well. You and me and Christian had a whole phial each before we even went out. Don't forget we had all that coke as well.'

'God, yeah, I still owe you for that. I better do some overtime this month to pay for it.' James drags himself to a wooden chair and sits down, conserving his energy for the while.

Venetia Latimer has been up and about since early this morning, watching some of the CCTV tapes that recorded the events in the grounds during last night's party. She finds them most instructive. Then she switches to the live camera and watches a couple of the kennel boys set off for Hampshire and Dorset in the van.

Venetia has suffered. She was once betrayed and robbed by someone she cared about. Venetia went into the tunnel of wretchedness and bitterness that everyone goes into when something like that happens but she came out the other side deciding to work through the pain by doing good deeds. Venetia Latimer now strives to turn useless things into useful things. She brings this about by combining her formidable skills with endless financial means.

Who, other than Venetia Latimer, would have had the idea of trapping and training the mink that were set free by animal rights activists and are now colonizing the countryside and interfering with the food chain? Mrs Latimer has a team working day and night to put together the first comedy circus routine starring performing mink. It is a difficult task because mink kill each other for sport and the supply of performers needs constant replacement. The kennel boys have been searching the English countryside for them with nets, stout leather gloves and – at their insistence – cricket boxes to protect their genitals.

Venetia Latimer is a busy woman. She doesn't have time to sit back and rest on her laurels, otherwise she would be feeling very proud of her achievements. From a very young age she has admired artists and performers and keenly felt the gap between their productive lives and hers. It is only now, past the age of fifty, that she has been able to see that she, too, can offer something good to the world – usefulness.

20

Hot Line

Sheila has thought it over carefully and she's sure that when she wears long, dangly earrings, the messages from the aliens are stronger. Consequently, she has been experimenting with other ways of enhancing the alien signals. The triangular caps she has made for her ears out of tinfoil seem to work very well. They are barely noticeable so long as she keeps her hair falling forward and doesn't brush it back over her face nervously when she talks, which she has a habit of doing.

Sheila gathers all her courage for the next stage of her search for Roy. The time has come to try and find out how she can contact his captors. She picks up the phone.

A bored young woman sits in a meagrely furnished office by the phone with an A4 pad of paper, leaning on a plastic wood-effect table. She wears grey flannel trousers and a grey V-necked jumper. You might suppose she had come straight to this office from school if she weren't five years too old to be wearing uniform. Her hand trembles slightly when the phone rings and she takes up her pen with very great care before she answers.

'Hello, Hot Line. What activity do you have to report?'

'I don't have anything to report. I'd like some information.'

'We don't give information about extraterrestrials, we collect it.'

'Do you know where I can get information?'

'We don't give information.'

'You won't even give me information about where to get information?'

'No.'

Sheila sighs and puts down the phone. The young woman, unseen at the other end of the line, makes a V sign at the receiver before she replaces it in the cradle. She stops up her pen and replaces it, unused, on the blank pages in front of her. Then she leans back on the table top again, inadvertently rubbing shiny patches on the elbows of her fashionable yet unremarkable wool and viscose mix jumper.

Sheila picks up the phone again and dials Alison. She takes a tangential approach to the subject of her phone call. 'Theatres are like people, sometimes,' she tells Alison. 'They can be ugly on the outside but able to convey beauty inside. Take the South Bank, for example. The buildings are hideous but the seats are comfortable, the view of the stage is good and the acoustics are great.'

'I don't really go to the theatre much.'

'You should. There always seems to be a message for me, when I go. The words speak to me. Do you know what I mean?'

'Songs are like that. The words always seem really personal to your situation. Like when you're in love or when you break up with someone. Suddenly every song you hear seems to express the emotion you're feeling.'

'Do you think that there's more to this idea of hidden messages than we realize?'

'What do you mean?'

'Do you think possibly it's a special way of communicating with us?'

'Oh yes, I think artists always hope to communicate something, whether it's through theatre or painting or music.'

'I think what I'm really trying to ask is whether that communication could be hijacked in some way.'

'By politicians?'

'By aliens.'

Alison, slumming her way through the conversation without paying too much attention to Sheila's questions or her own responses, now tries to backtrack in her mind to see if she's missed out a chunk of the conversation and hasn't quite followed Sheila's meaning.

'Um. Aliens.'

'I think that aliens have been communicating with me through the medium of theatre. I know it sounds strange.'

'Yes, it does.'

'I feel so powerless. I feel as if Roy is standing just the other side of a door and I can't see him. I need someone to help me but when I come up against snotty people like the woman on the Extraterrestrial Hot Line, all the breath is knocked out of me and I feel as if I can't get started. It makes me feel very alone. Don't you ever feel lonely, Alison?'

'No.'

After she has hung up, Alison walks around the flat for a while, thinking about Sheila, then she takes a poem with a phone number written on it from a noticeboard on the wall above her computer and goes back to the phone.

'Jeff?'

'Ali?'

'Thanks for the lip gloss. I thought I might come and visit you. I could cook something for you. Everything would be brightly coloured and fragrant.'

'You said you had a lot of colour in your life.'

'I'd make a salad and scatter it with flower petals. I'd build a pyramid from scoops of melon soaked in vodka. I'd use watermelon, cantaloupe, honeydew – red, yellow and orange. Then I'd add some green from little twists of lime and mint picked from my garden.'

'And you'd cook them?'

'I wasn't actually going to apply heat to them, no. I suppose it isn't cooking so much as assembling and balancing fruit.'

'When will you visit me?'

'I wonder if it would be a good idea or a bad idea if I came to visit you? I don't think I could sleep next to you. I'd just lie awake listening to you breathing. It's a habit I've got into with Phoebe.'

'I think it would be a good idea.'

'I could bring my mobile with me. Taron would be able to tell me.'

It is two o'clock in the afternoon. The bright light outside reaches into the corners of Jane Memory's bedroom and intensifies the vivid green and blue of the large checks on the expensive cotton covers and pillowcases on the bed, where Jeremy is lying without any clothes on. Jeremy's tan line stops two inches below his navel, approximately where a pair of hipster trousers would begin, if he ever wore them.

Jane used to bite her nails when she was a teenager and her manicurist uses extensions in natural pink to disguise the damage that remains. Jane uses the acrylic tip of one these nails to tap Jeremy gently on the ribs, signalling that he should roll over. She rests her silver-ringed hand in a fan shape on one white buttock and inspects the rest of Jeremy's body. It is very lean. She pinches a little bit of skin between her thumb and first finger. He probably has no more than 14 or 15 per cent fat on him.

'Ow', says Jeremy.

Jane puts her mouth to his shoulder and smells the skin before she bites him, sweeping her hand between his thighs. He turns over so that she can sit on top of him, the soles of her feet tucked under the backs of his legs and her hands at either side of him on the blue and green checked pillows under his head.

A shower of shiny, golden pound coins has fallen from the hip pockets of Jeremy's summer dress into the bed, as if riches have flowed directly from his loins. Every so often Jane or Jeremy rolls on to one of the coins, gasps, and throws it on to the floor where it bounces against the skirting board with a 'ting'.

There is no part of Jane's body that she dislikes. She exfoliates her knees and her elbows regularly. Her nipples point up, her buttocks point up, her hips are narrow, her stomach is flat. There is a clear, straight line of vision from her breastbone to her pubic bone, with nothing wobbly in the way. She might get her belly button pierced, but she's not convinced it won't hurt. If she got sick of it and removed it, she'd hate it to leave a scar.

'Oh,' says Jeremy. 'God, Jane.'

Jane leans forward with one hand against the wall behind his head and dips her head so she can kiss him. If they shower together it will save time and she can drop Jeremy back at his flat before the rush hour traffic begins, unless he insists on travelling back there by bicycle, in which case she can probably have sex with him again and still have enough time to pop into Marks and Spencer to pick up something for her dinner.

Jane's boyfriend Philippe Noir has square feet with a high instep. His fingers are rectangular. His hands, like his feet, are slightly moist, even in the cold weather. He has full lips, which is supposed to be an indication of sensuality, although he displays none of this when in bed with Jane. When they first spent time together, Jane would bring pots of strawberry fromage frais or vanilla ice cream to bed and leave them where they were easily to hand in case Philippe should feel the urge to slather her body with it and flick it away with his thick pink tongue. He preferred to finish eating the food – one spoon for you, one for me; he has always been fair about sharing it – while she grasped his cock and said 'umm' a lot to get him in the mood.

Philippe likes to keep abreast of developments in the competitive docu-soap world and schedules their lovemaking so that there is plenty of time to sit up in bed, find his designer glasses with thick rectangular frames wherever he has discarded them, and switch on the TV for the next edition of a rival's work. The thing about Philippe is that he doesn't really have to try very hard as he has a good job and could always get another girlfriend if he wanted one.

Since Jeremy insists on getting himself home on his bicycle this afternoon, Jane has enough time to have sex with him again. She lies him on the floor, ties him to the wooden feet of the bed by the wrists with a pair of her knickers (she makes a kind of slipknot with the leg holes), tucks a cushion under his arse so he doesn't get carpet burns, and tips some of the most delicious contents of her freezer over his body and licks it off. Jane often eats in restaurants with friends so there isn't much to choose from but she manages to take Jeremy through the full range of emotions using a tub of frozen blackberry yoghurt, a bottle of frozen but still viscous Absolut vodka and a tray of ice cubes. He wobbles a little unsteadily on his bicycle when the time comes to leave, but whether this is due to the alcohol or the sex, Jane couldn't say.

21

Wind Chimes

Sheila wakes groggily to a terrible thumping sound. She is not sure at first whether there is someone at the door or whether the noise is inside her head. Since Roy's disappearance she has been suffering from headaches. Unless she rests, the headaches get worse and eventually she has to close her eyes to bright lights and spots of colour that she sees jumping across her vision, even though she knows they are not there. Her sister would say it is stress.

'Sheila?' Her sister is at the door now, calling her name. Bang, bang, bang, bang, bang, bang, bang. The woman has fists of steel. 'Sheila?' Bang, bang, bang, tap, tap, tap. Tap, tap, tap. Bang, bang, bang.

Sheila waits until her sister has gone. The phone starts to ring but she doesn't answer it. Ring ring. Ring ring. Ring ring. Ring ring. Ring ring. After five rings it rolls over onto the answer machine.

Sheila gets out of bed and checks the message, in case it is not from her sister. It is, though. Above her head, on the table where she keeps the phone, there hangs an unusual wind chime made from recycled cutlery that she bought recently from Covent Garden market. When the tines of the forks strike against the bowls of the spoons and the blades of the knives, there is a very pretty 'ding' sound.

It is rare that a breeze stirs within Sheila's flat as she prefers to keep her windows closed against the traffic noise. However, the primary purpose of the contraption is to gather and concentrate messages from aliens so on the whole Sheila is very pleased with her purchase and the frown lines in her face relax a little whenever she passes it in her hallway.

Roy has climbed the wooden ladder leading to Sylvia's high wire, now more or less permanently strung in place, and is standing on the platform next to the house, looking out over the small bay. To the left, past the orchard, he can see the top of the hay barn, a maroon structure the size of an aircraft hangar. The land behind him is hidden from view by the house. He still dislikes heights but by climbing up here often and just looking around, he is coming to terms with the feelings of dizziness and disorientation that come from being so far above the ground.

When Roy was a child he thought that Heaven would be familiar, like a sunny England. During his difficult teenage years, he didn't believe in the afterlife. As an adult he thought Heaven would be exotic and unfamiliar, the sort of place that is unattainable for ordinary people, like Richard Branson's island in the Caribbean.

This morning, as he walked along the path leading to the beach, he noticed hundreds and hundreds of cobwebs in the hedgerows, each strand of each web sparkling with drops of moisture from the mist that had come in from the sea. By the time he went to fetch Sylvia to show her how magical it looked, the mist had rolled back and the cobwebs had shed the moisture, their patterns barely noticeable among the leaves as they had been every other morning that Roy had walked along the path. If it weren't for magic like this, Roy could almost be disappointed in how much Heaven is like the English country-side of his childhood.

22

The Café

Venetia Latimer is feeling lonely. On days like these, bitterness can creep up on her unless she takes care not to let it in. Her husband is at work, her son has left home. She has a business of her own to run, but still the bitter feelings ambush her in the quiet moments when she is alone in her office.

Venetia is thinking about the money Sylvia took from her. She had shown Sylvia the grey suitcase filled with money that she kept in the safe for emergencies and contingencies, and she had shown her the safe combination. Sylvia was a very open and unaffected person, she didn't shy away from intimacy or confidences. Venetia always felt she could truly be herself in front of Sylvia – truly an idiot, in the case of the suitcase full of money.

Sylvia let her do little things for her, which Venetia enjoyed. Sylvia said it reminded her of the way the girls used to take care of each other in the circus. Venetia washed Sylvia's hair for her, and she plaited it sometimes, deftly and tightly as if preparing a horse for a show. Venetia painted Sylvia's fingernails, she helped her with her tax return, she made sure Sylvia had custard to go with her puddings in the evenings if she wanted it. There was no part of Sylvia's life that she didn't care about.

Venetia would like to recover the elephant Sylvia stole from her and she would like to recover the money. She would like to open the suitcase and then destroy it in front of Sylvia, burning it or tearing the twenty-pound notes into shreds, scrunching the pieces and letting them run through her fingers to show that it wasn't just about the money after all. It was about something else she lost when Sylvia ran away.

I must work through the pain, thinks Venetia Latimer. She breathes in very deeply once, then again, to activate her brain with oxygen. I must make my mark on the world and leave it a better place. She turns to her Usefulness file.

On a personal level, Mrs Latimer's quest to turn the useless into the useful extends its reach into her son Joey's life. Miss Lester's dating agency literature and Taron's phone number are listed in Joey's section of the Usefulness file. She would like to prevent Joey from working in the City and she would like to find him a girlfriend with rings on her fingers and bells on her toes. Someone with lots of eyeliner and an unconventional attitude to life. Someone like Taron. Although she is currently focused on finding the right girl for Joey, Mrs Latimer would be equally enthusiastic about finding him the right man if he ever were to ask for her help in this area. She only wants to save him from a life of well-cut suits and conservatism. However, Mrs Latimer belongs to a generation who associate gay men with wide lapels and saucy double entendres and she might be appalled to discover that homosexuality and conservatism are not mutually exclusive.

Among the other Usefulness projects, the performing mink are coming along well. Venetia has also recently written to the head teachers of all the local primary schools in the area suggesting that, since pre-teen children are reportedly concerned about the environment and particularly about litter, they should be provided with small-sized rubber gloves made from recycled materials and asked to collect a bag of rubbish each on their way to school. She doesn't know that children don't walk to school any more. Their mothers drop them at the school gates in their Volvos.

There is another, still nebulous, project which Venetia has been formulating. It could benefit men, and in turn all mankind, but it is unlikely it will come to fruition in her lifetime. Nevertheless it may be something she can use to advance the plans she has to ruin Mrs Fitzgerald. Venetia Latimer dwells for a moment on vengeance, which, like her projects for usefulness and like time, will heal her wounds. Then she goes to meet Mrs Fitzgerald.

Ella Fitzgerald is waiting for Venetia Latimer in a small café near Clapham Junction, where they have agreed to meet. Small pieces of other people's food crunch underfoot as Mrs Fitzgerald takes her place at a table near the window and looks around. The siren smell of bacon cooking apparently induces the regular customers to eat whatever is put in front of them in spite of the unhygienic surrounds.

Mrs Fitzgerald flicks a very small fragment of a previous occupant's charred bacon from where her hands rest on the table to a cosier spot between the tomato sauce bottle and the sugar shaker. She orders a large cappuccino and an apricot Danish, and she settles to watch the people around her.

Almost everyone else in the café is a solitary diner, catching up on their calories, lost in their thoughts. There is something – perhaps it is the harsh hospital lighting and the plastic seats, or the way that the café's occupants pour over the *Sun* newspaper rather than connecting with each other – that makes Mrs Fitzgerald feel very lonely. If there were a waiting room where people took their places to turn mad, it would look like this: the table tops smeared with ketchup; the people sitting close to each other but apart, drinking no-brand cola and eating black pudding with chips, wearing layers of jewellery fashioned in thinly beaten gold, as if to pay a Stygian keeper of the gates of madness. The café is comfortable, warm and smelly, but to Mrs Fitzgerald it is a staging post on the frontier between sanity and madness.

Venetia Latimer takes her place across the table, ready for the showdown. Mrs Fitzgerald signals for the boy to take her companion's order, then plays it straight.

'I've been investigating your organization.'

'I know.'

'You've been feeding a prototype veterinary drug called Serum Ten to your animals. Emphglott, your sponsor, supplies you with all your food and the serum.'

'You've found no evidence of maltreatment or illegal activity.'

'No maltreatment. Your work with Emphglott is unethical. Your relationship with them is not good business practice.'

'You've found nothing. I'm sure you feel your methods are thorough and yet you've found nothing.'

'I have found two areas of concern and that's why I've asked to meet you. Firstly, can you explain the disappearance of an elephant? Secondly, can you explain why you've also been feeding Serum Ten to your employees?'

Mrs Latimer swirls her teaspoon in her tea and looks at Mrs Fitzgerald for a moment. 'I have a proposal for you. The animals in my care are well loved and well looked after. That is your main concern and you agree that I have met all your standards?'

'Yes.'

'While you've been investigating me, I've been investigating you. I like you, Mrs Fitzgerald, and I have nothing to fear from you.'

'Very well.'

'One of your investigators has been working for the wife of one of my employees, trying to trace him since his disappearance. I've been paying the bills so you've been working for me indirectly. You may know that already.'

'Yes.'

'I would like to hire you to trace another missing person, which is linked to the disappearance of the elephant, Sorrel. If you accept, I will tell you about Serum Ten, on the understanding that any information I give you must be protected by client privilege, as rigorously as if information were passing between a solicitor and a client.'

'Very well. In that case let me set out my position clearly. Any information you may give me that falls within the remit of my original investigation into the welfare of your animals, I will act upon. I will respect the confidentiality of any other information, unless it is illegal or unethical, in which case I will use my judgement and act accordingly.'

'I respect your judgement. Here's my story. My business relationship with Emphglott is very rewarding. They supply me with dog food in return for publicity. They sponsor the dog shows I enter and win. I win on merit, every time, but they are my sponsors nevertheless. The relationship is close, I accept that, but I'm doing nothing wrong by exploiting it.

'Emphglott developed Serum Ten and had to abandon trials when they proved inconclusive. I agreed to continue to trial it, unofficially, together with its upgraded version, Serum Eleven. Serum Eleven hasn't been trialled anywhere so its presence won't have been picked up by any lab you've asked to investigate. Neither substance is banned in Britain. OK so far?'

'Yes.' Mrs Fitzgerald nibbles at her Danish pastry and signals the boy for another cappuccino.

'I think it's increasingly hard for men to find a role in society, don't you agree?'

'I'm sorry?'

'You and I, Mrs Fitzgerald, we are successful business women. Everywhere you look, there are successful women.' Mrs Latimer's gestures, their theatricality restricted by the environment, take in a greasy youth reading the *Sun* and an elderly man eating scrambled egg from a yellow plate with cracked enamelling. 'Men have nothing more relevant to offer society than inane commentaries on football, or a fight after a skinful of lager on a Saturday night.'

Mrs Fitzgerald, still nibbling, thinks of Jeremy Paxman, Tony Blair, Bill Gates, Damien Hirst and the Archbishop of Canterbury. She thinks of Gary Barlow, Ted Hughes, Stephen King and Quentin Tarantino.

'Single-parent families are the norm, these days. Women are perfectly capable of bringing up children alone. We need men to provide us with sperm, that's all.' Mrs Fitzgerald colours slightly at 'us'. 'Soon, in twenty years or so, we won't even need them to breed. Scientists will be able to manufacture sperm. We need to find a role for men in the future. All this has a bearing on what I'm about to tell you, Mrs Fitzgerald.'

'Why have you allowed your employees access to Serum Ten and Eleven?'

'At first it was a mistake, of course. Some of the kennel lads have been experimenting with the animals' drugs. It's one of the hazards of modern working life. People who work in offices pilfer stationery and pens. People who work with animals steal their food and medication. It has some kind of psychotropic effect, heightening their awareness of colour. It stimulates the release of serotonins so they are very cheerful all the time. I noticed that it modified their behaviour. They are more pleasant, more docile and well-behaved. I'd like to find a way to manufacture it in large quantities and trial it only on men. I need to work with a woman I can trust, someone with business experience who also understands the way things work on, um, the street. We could sell it at football matches and check its effect on crowd aggression. With findings as valuable as this, we could be famous.'

We? Is Mrs Latimer inviting Mrs Fitzgerald to join with her in dealing drugs at football matches as some kind of social science experiment? Mrs Fitzgerald, whose lifelong struggle has been to seek justice for people and liberty for animals, is being invited to participate in this . . . madness.

'You knowingly allowed your employees to experiment with these substances?'

'It was amazing, given a period of time for the effects to develop. The men became more docile and obedient. Like pets. That's my breakthrough. That's the role for men for the future. We can keep them as pets.'

'The differences between the species were blurred, so that the dogs became more like men and the men became more like dogs?'

'Men need to become smaller, softer, cleaner, more docile. If they were to be kept as pets, their world would shrink, possibly to the four walls of a single girl's flat in town, with a walk in a park or an outing to a pub once a day, so they would need to be unquestioning of their surroundings.'

'Men as pets?'

'Remember, Mrs Fizgerald, this is an extraordinary break-through. You must respect my need for discretion.'

'Have you had any of your findings verified?'

'It's almost impossible. I haven't measured the doses taken by the men. I haven't documented what they were like before the changes – how do you measure changes like that? I haven't got a control group. I know I'm doing it all wrong. All I have is the idea, a vision for the future. I do like men, don't you? I'd hate to see a world without them. This is a way to help them survive the future.'

'What was the original use for the drug?'

'It was supposed to make the dogs more docile and more adaptable to their confined conditions and therefore easier to handle.'

'Is any of this connected to your missing person inquiry?'

'No. A woman who used to work for me stole fifteen thousand pounds and the elephant from me. I want you to help me find her and recover the money. There's a large bonus in it if you do so.'

'I'll take the missing person inquiry. Have you tried to find this woman before?'

'Yes. When Sylvia first disappeared I hired a private detective but he couldn't find her. That's what happens when you ask a man to do something important, they're useless. I'd do it myself but I don't know where to start.'

'I think, if I may say so, that the other detective merely approached this the wrong way. It can be very difficult to find one person among nearly sixty million people, especially if they don't wish to be found. However, if we treat this as a missing elephant inquiry, everything becomes much simpler. Sylvia must be obtaining specialist supplies and medical care for the elephant and we can find her through that.'

'That's very astute. And you're right about Sorrel. She will be eating up to forty pounds of hay and forty-five pounds of fruit and vegetables a day by now and unless Sylvia is growing these herself, she'll be buying them somewhere.'

'I have an operative who can get to work on it straightaway. As for your other proposition, I'll get back to you.'

23

Bandits

Taron and her friend Joey Latimer are crouching by the side of the road, surrounded by coloured plastic pails of water, handkerchiefs tied over mouth and nose, like bandits. Joey has pushed a hollow tube between the roots of a roadside tree and Taron is filling it with water, watching the level slowly sink, then filling it again. They are absorbed in their task, like children making mud pies, their fingers grimy from the dust thrown up by the passing traffic. Hugo Fragrance, in his City suit in his lunch hour, stands awkwardly to one side, holding a bucket and a sponge as if between bouts at a boxing match.

'One thousand cars pass along the Limehouse link every quarter of an hour when the traffic is at its busiest,' Taron tells Hugo.

'Have you heard about carbon neutrality?' he asks Taron. 'You can get someone to calculate how much damage you're doing to the ozone layer and then you can buy trees to compensate. The theory is that the trees repair the damage, eventually.'

'It's like a penance,' says Joey. 'Like rich people buying prayers for their immortal souls.'

'Really?' says Taron. She removes the handkerchief so they can see she is saying it scornfully.

As Taron waits for the bus home, her mother calls her on her mobile phone. 'Are you feeling OK?'

'Yes.'

'I feel terrible. I wonder if it's the leftover chicken satay you brought round from that party the other night. It's playing havoc with my psychic abilities. Whose party was it?'

'My friend Joey's mother's.'

'Is he your boyfriend?'

'No.'

'I keep seeing a man standing on a platform, high above the ground. I feel that he's facing some sort of danger.'

'Is it a diving platform?'

'Let me think. No, I don't think so. He's got his clothes on.'

'Who is he?'

'I don't know.'

'Well, it must mean something to someone. I'll ask around. Thanks for the warning.'

In her flat in Brixton, Sheila is waiting in vain for another message about Roy. The Sky satellite dish installed outside the house, the forest of television aerials inside, the cutlery wind chimes above the phone, the sheets of tinfoil at the windows, all have had no noticeable effect for several days. Wearily, Sheila removes a tinfoil cap from one ear and reaches for the phone to call Alison. She tells her about the advertisement she has seen in the window of the newsagent's shop on Brixton Hill:

CLOSE ENCOUNTERS GROUP
SHARE INFORMATION ABOUT EXTRATERRESTRIALS
MEETING EVERY THURSDAY 6.30 P.M.

When Thursday comes, Alison and Sheila are there. The

meeting is held in a private room on the third floor in St Matthew's Church in Brixton.

Alison and Sheila do not remove their coats, they sit on plastic chairs at the back of the room and try to follow the proceedings.

'Dolphins are much cleverer than humans,' asserts a woman wearing a maroon cardigan. She emphasizes all the nouns in her sentences as if worried that her listeners will be unable to follow the key points she is trying to make. The effort makes her drawl. 'Dolphin speech patterns have been developed to communicate with aliens. They keep talking to humans because they're waiting for us to catch up with them and understand what they're telling us.'

'Sounds like typical English tourists,' whispers Alison, cheerfully.

'Wherever there are dolphins, there is alien activity. That's why there are so many of them in the oceans near California and Mexico. It's also where the majority of spaceships have been spotted, and where most abductions are reported.'

A man in a Nike sweatshirt and Reebok trainers gets to his feet. 'We need to follow the example of our ancestors and attract the attention of extraterrestrials with diagrams and patterns large enough to be seen from their spaceships. Did you realize that there are prehistoric stone formations in the desert that can still be seen from the air? If we want aliens to make contact, we have to be just as persistent as our ancestors. We have to let them know we're here and we want to talk to them.'

'The Millennium Dome would be a good place to hang out, if you wanted them to see you,' offers a thin man in his twenties with a cowslick in his dark hair. He, too is wearing sports clothing, although he favours Adidas. Everyone looks at him as if he's an idiot, so he sits down again.

'Does anyone have any questions?' asks the woman in the

maroon cardigan. Alison leans across Sheila's lap and then leans back again, having satisfied herself that the woman is wearing jogging pants and trainers.

Sheila stands up, bends to place her handbag at her feet, then straightens and addresses the room. 'If we were going to build a diagram to attract a spaceship, where would we build it?'

'In a field.'

'On a ley line.'

'On a beach,' says the woman in the maroon cardigan, with authority. 'Is anyone interested in doing it? What picture shall we make?'

'A crocodile.'

'A hunter.'

'A circle.'

'A face,' says Sheila, bending again and taking a photocopied poster from her handbag. 'My husband, Roy. I think they've taken him.'

'You want to construct a missing persons advertisement, featuring your husband's face?'

'Yes.'

Sheila's proposal seems to go down very well with the assembled company, generating an excitement that breaks down the awkwardness and inhibitions between the group members, whose defence of entrenched positions (dolphins, prehistoric man, Millennium Dome) is apparently part of an ongoing weekly battle.

'We could plot the face on a graph and use light and dark stones to build up the likeness and shade in the features,' suggests the lad with the cowslick.

'It would be like using pixels on a computer image,' enthuses the man wearing Reeboks.

'Or a knitting pattern.'

'Like Myra Hindley's face made from children's handprints.'
Alison has not yet entered into the spirit of the meeting.

'I'm Rosy,' says the woman in the cardigan.

'Sheila.'

'Come to our meeting, same time next week, and we'll plan
the picture.'

'I'll collect the car and bring it round to the front,' Alison tells
Sheila, 'and then I'll drop you home. I'll give you a shout when
I'm ready, yeah?'

'There's no need to shout, I can hear you perfectly well.'

'Alison?'

'Taron? Whenever I think about you, you ring me.'

'Beware of a man on a high platform.'

'Are you still off the drugs?'

'Yes. Although it turns out that I ingested some animal
tranquillizers at that party the other week. I think I may have
hallucinated the Doberman reading the newspaper. Sorry about
that, I hope it didn't affect your report on Joey's mother.'

'Never mind, I didn't really believe you anyway. What's this
about a platform?'

'My mother's been having visions. Look out for a man on a
platform. I suppose it could be someone about to jump. Check
out the bridges whenever you cross the river to go into town.
That's what I'm doing. I'll let you know if I see anything.'

24

Dry White Wine

Mrs Fitzgerald is reading *Monica's Story* on the 137 bus. Reading while sitting in a moving vehicle always makes her feel queasy. Today is no exception. Mrs Fitzgerald fears for Monica's mental health. She pities even those who court fame, especially the young. How can they understand the irreversible impact it will have on their lives? 'Never, never, never, never,' says Mrs Fitzgerald aloud, her hanky at her lips. She feels as if the tentacles of the world's press extend so widely that any innocent woman, even herself, might be in danger of brushing against them and getting spun into some whirlpool of notoriety. Her head is full of sea monster and whirlpool, Scylla and Charybdis. She seems unaware that she is making a groaning sound as she shows her Travelcard to the conductor.

Miss Lester and Jane Memory are a bit tipsy. They are drinking dry white wine in a wine bar at Miss Lester's expense.

Jane is looking round for a waiter and holding a conversation with Miss Lester at the same time. 'I think, don't you, that we're all quite empty inside. This dating agency of yours is a sign of the times. We're part of a generation – well, I call it the Doughnut Generation – we're part of a generation that's disappointed with life.'

'Yes.'

'So you have prostitutes mingling with your clients at the dating agency?'

'Yes.'

'Are any of them transsexuals?'

'No.'

'Are you?'

'No.'

'I really don't think this story is going anywhere. I'm looking for something I can pitch for network TV.'

'Oh yes, Jane, you'd be able to spend a bit on your hair.'

'Yes, madam?' The waiter is here at last.

Jane Memory earns £45,000 per year plus expenses. She does her hair at home because she doesn't want to pay the money to a hairdresser, not because she can't pay. 'Another bottle of wine, please.'

'I thought you might be able to expand on your doughnut theory and interview some of my clients, with their permission of course.'

'Thank you. I'm afraid there are so many empty people in London that I have no shortage of subjects.'

'Oh well, it doesn't matter. I really don't like the genuine customers very much. The women are so desperate and the men are so crass. There is no tenderness or humanity in them. I much prefer the prostitutes. There is someone I'd like you to meet – Ella Fitzgerald, she runs a detective agency. She's not empty at all; quite the opposite. She's a very inspirational force – grand, capable and reassuring.'

'Is she middle-aged? Maybe I could do something as part of my empire builder series. They do some lovely photos. I see her alone on stage, blinking in a spotlight, sequinned dress, noticeably past her prime. We could play with the idea that she

follows and exposes people and we could expose her vulnerabi-
lity.'

'Sequins?'

'It would be better than photographing her in a Dick Tracey
outfit, wouldn't it?'

'Well, if that's the choice. Maybe I should speak to her first.'

25

Anthropolgists

Roy has placed a garden hose in a straight line on the ground. One end stretches out towards the sea. The other end leads back towards the tap on the standpipe in the elephant's quarters, where it is usually attached.

Arms wide, at shoulder height, Roy slowly places one foot before the other along its length. He is concentrating on balancing, on feeling that he can walk on a thin rope. He is dead. If he falls off the rope he cannot kill himself and yet when he steps off the platform for the first time, he wants Sylvia to know that he is trying to do it right.

'A geography student came to the door last night trying to raise sponsorship money for a project he wants to join,' Sheila tells Alison. 'About a dozen of them are going abroad, including geologists, anthropologists and marine biologists. They're going to map uncharted territories and learn about the people there. He spent quite a lot of time explaining it and he left me some literature.'

'Did you give him any money?'

'I gave him twenty pounds. I've been thinking about it all night. It has made me look differently at the space around me.

Have you seen those police notices everywhere appealing for witnesses to crimes, with the date and time they were carried out?'

'The yellow boards?'

'Yes, they're about three feet high, in tall, narrow tent shapes. The police put them as near as possible to the spot where a crime has happened. I walked past one this morning on the way to the paper shop. It makes it look as if the whole area has been labelled. If you leave aside that the police are involved, it looks as if the notices have been put there to guide anthropologists exploring the neighbourhood. I started to think, maybe they really are signs, and maybe there are others left around unobtrusively so that Londoners going about their daily lives won't think twice about them.'

'When you look at it that way, there are signs everywhere in London if you think about all the graffiti and posters.'

'There are also sensory ones for smell and hearing, as if the labellers have never met the anthropologists and they aren't really sure how to present the information to make it most useful to them.'

'Every time you walk on a path in London you have to do that dog shit dance, trying to avoid the steaming piles dotted everywhere. I suppose it might be easier to bear if it hadn't just been left there indiscriminately, lying warm and stinking right where it's dropped from a dog's arse. Do you think dog shit could be there for a reason, Sheila?'

'What about the drum and bass music that comes from the open windows of the houses and flats? That could be a signal of some kind. It might serve the same purpose as fishermen banging on the hulls of their boats to attract fish. And then there are the cars driving round and round a small area playing equally loud music. It's as if there are squads of counter-agents trying to create confusion by obliterating the music signposts coming from the houses.'

'But who are these signs for, Sheila?'

'They could be aimed at anthropologists from outer space.'

'Well, that's one possible explanation.'

26

Plague of Blonde Women

Venetia Latimer sits in her living room with her feet on an ottoman and tries to put flesh on the bones of her scheme to entrap Mrs Fitzgerald. The meeting at the café went well. Mrs Fitzgerald appeared intrigued by her ideas about testing the serum on football crowds. Now Venetia has to come up with a viable plan that will hook Mrs Fitzgerald and lead her into the hands of the law.

Mrs Latimer likes the geographical complexities of selling drugs at football matches. She can appear to implicate herself by pretending she is the other side of London selling to a rival team – 'You take Chelsea, Ella, I'll cover the Arsenal' – without raising Mrs Fitzgerald's suspicions. Unfortunately she has never been to a football match and her plan stalls in the detail. Do drug dealers frequent the local pubs at football matches or do they stand right outside the grounds looking as if they have something to sell? The plan is too sketchy and an experienced operator like Mrs Fitzgerald will never bite. Which other area of life is predominated by males? Venetia Latimer sighs. Which isn't?

Possibly Mrs Fitzgerald could be persuaded to sell the drugs in City pubs. If she had any success, the effects might be interesting. Trading would slacken as the traders, their aggression curbed by the serum, tried to reach deals with each other that accommodated both sides.

Even better, Mrs Fitzgerald might agree to set up a hot line from her office to supply the serum. It would be perfectly plausible to explain that she cannot use her own phone number in case it is recognized by Stephen or Joey or their colleagues.

Venetia Latimer reaches for the phone and calls the *News of the World* to sound out their interest in the story. She reaches the honey trap team.

'I can supply evidence that a London private detective is selling drugs in the City. Will you run the story if I play Linda Tripp to her Monica?'

The tired journalist places the phone receiver on the desk and shouts, 'Lady with a drugs story about a harmonica. Any takers?' There are none. His colleagues are gathered at a desk near the window, reviewing a muddle of photographs of a nude sports hero smoking crack in the presence of one of the newspaper's reporters.

The journalist offers to take the skeleton details of the story from Mrs Latimer over the phone but it is not long before he interrupts. 'The problem, madam, is that you are telling me that this person is selling dog tranquillizers to City traders. It is not illegal to sell drugs unless they are banned substances. I'm afraid it won't make the front pages.'

Mrs Latimer gets up and walks around her living room, momentarily stumped. She vows she will not rest until she gets Mrs Fitzgerald's licence revoked, however tiresome the process of making this happen. Mrs Fitzgerald must be punished. There is nothing else for Venetia Latimer to do but to obtain an illegal substance and add it to the phials of serum before passing it to Mrs Fitzgerald for sale in the City.

As Jeremy opens the lid of the suitcase, even before Jane sees the piles of used purple twenty-pound notes stacked neatly in rows on the left side of the grey lining, she catches the elemental smell that used money has – metallic, like soil.

'Why is the money just on one side of the suitcase?'

'Well, I've spent the money that was on the other side. I take what I need, going along the rows, top to bottom, right to left. I don't see the point in rearranging it just to make it symmetrical. Sylvia gave it to me before she ran away. She asked me to pay someone to investigate her employer. There's so much money here that I've been able to use some of it to fund the traffic campaign.'

'What's the investigation?'

'Sylvia wanted to ensure the animals she'd been working with weren't being ill-treated after she left. Personally, I think it's all right to make a profit from animals if you feed them properly and exercise them.'

'Are the animals being ill-treated?'

'I don't know. I try not to get involved. I drop off the money anonymously and collect a monthly report from a post office box to forward to Sylvia so that the detective agency can't trace the money back to her. I saw the agency boss on a bus once. She looked straight at me, as if she knew me.'

'Guilty people always think everyone else knows their secrets. Did you see any of the reports?'

'Why?'

'I'm always looking for stories. Animals make good telly. Come on, Jeremy, help me out here.'

'Why don't you ask her what's going on yourself? The agency's only down in Brixton. I'll give you the address if you like.'

In Sainsbury's in Clapham Park Road, Ella Fitzgerald is approached by a tall, cadaverous blonde woman wearing wraparound mirrored sunglasses that barely disguise the sappy bruises on her face.

'Can you help me get some food?' The woman refuses the two one-pound coins Mrs Fitzgerald offers her. 'I've got money. Can you help me buy the food? I don't know what to get. I haven't eaten for three days.' The woman sways unsteadily on her feet. Her words are beautifully enunciated in a deep voice, like Joanna Lumley's.

'A sandwich?' suggests Mrs Fitzgerald, moved by the woman's helplessness and her perfect diction. 'Tuna and sweetcorn? Cheese and pickle?'

'I'm vegan.'

'An avocado, then. Bananas.' Mrs Fitzgerald steers her round the fruit and vegetable section, loading a small basket. 'Bread rolls. Do you have any cutlery? Do you have anything to eat the food with? Crisps? Some chocolate for energy?'

'I'm macrobiotic.' The woman's arm shoots out suddenly and grabs a bottle of white wine on special offer, clutching it close to her chest while Mrs Fitzgerald struggles with the basket. The woman produces a ten-pound note at the till.

'Have you got a reward card?' asks the check-out assistant.

'No.'

'Would you like one?' The assistant, avoiding eye contact, hasn't seen the oozing bruises or the urgency with which the woman plucks the wine bottle from the conveyor belt.

'I'm in a hurry.'

Unaccustomed to driving in Brixton, Jane nevertheless quickly adapts to the local custom that permits those travelling in a moving vehicle to change road position without signalling. Until evolution grows a third hand on Brixton car drivers, they are fully occupied with one hand clamped to the mobile phone at their ear, while using no more than two fingers of the other hand to lightly steer past the dented saloon cars parked along the high street. If they are eating a sandwich while talking on the phone, they sometimes have to steer with one elbow, which takes a great deal of skill. As well as being unable to signal, there is little opportunity for Brixton drivers to change gear when their hands are occupied, and consequently they aim to maintain a constant speed in third gear.

All the most convenient parking positions in the bus lanes are already taken by the time Jane arrives in the high street. Cars and vans are parked along the red route and the double yellow lines on Coldharbour Lane, reducing it to a single duo-directional lane of traffic. Jane leaves the car in Tesco's car park and walks the short distance to a doorway past McDonald's, from where she can observe Mrs Fitzgerald's office window. It's an uncomfortable place to stand in the middle of the morning as the young mothers with pre-school children are out in force, bumping their children's legs on the pushchairs and slapping them without warning, presumably to prepare them for the pain of separation once they are old enough to be handed over to state education.

Somewhat shaken by the encounter in Sainsbury's, Mrs Fitzgerald crosses Brixton High Street hurriedly, raising her handbag to hide her face as she tucks into the doorway leading to her first-floor office, where she calls Alison over to the window.

'Do you see that woman near McDonald's?'

'The tall blonde with sunglasses?'

'There seems to be a plague of pallid blonde women in the area. Will you hand me the binoculars?'

'She's looking this way. Do you think she's watching us?'

'I thought it might be the woman from the supermarket but it isn't. She's dressed more smartly and she's less damaged.'

'Do you think she's part of some counter-surveillance operation?'

'She has a pair of binoculars trained on our window.'

'Maybe she's interested in the dinner dating agency. Miss Lester seems to be courting publicity for it.'

'Alison, I'd like to avoid exposure to any kind of publicity.' Mrs Fitzgerald shudders as she folds the strap of the binoculars and puts them into their case. She thinks of Gazza and Tony Adams MBE and Paul Merson, struggling with demons caused by the pressures of being in the public eye. She thinks of poor Tara Palmer-Tomkinson.

'Imagine how it would feel to be watched all the time, Alison. I should hate to be famous. There is no rest from the intrusion. I have heard people say that if you desire fame then you should expect the press to spy on you and ambush you to take more photos.'

'It's an argument that's difficult to refute.'

'There is no other job where if you commit a certain amount of your time to one kind of activity, for example having your picture taken or giving interviews to the press, you are deemed to have somehow lost the right to stop doing that activity the rest of the time. It's as spurious as saying that a woman who walks down the street in lipstick and a short skirt is "asking for it", or that if a woman has sexual relations with one man then she should be prepared to be pestered for sex from other men. It is about control, respect and the right to privacy.'

'You're right. If a ski instructor comes off the slopes at six p.m. people on skis don't spend the rest of the night ducking in front of him shouting, "What do I do now?" trying to trick him into giving skiing lessons. If an accountant is on a family picnic on a Sunday afternoon you don't get proprietors of small businesses launching themselves from the undergrowth and insisting on having their books balanced.'

'Exactly. If a person is famous, they don't stop being a person. The fame should not be an excuse for anyone to be harassed, bullied and sneered at. We are all trying to get by in our own way, even famous people.'

27

Sylvia's Flip-Flop

A torn piece of a poster washes up onto the shore, wrapping around Sylvia's flip-flop as she walks by the sea very early in the morning, before tending to the elephant.

'*Personne Disparue. Est-ce que vous avez vu cette personne?*'

Some French people have lost someone they love. Sylvia pulls at the paper to free it from her foot and it disintegrates in her hands. She scrunches it up like papier-mâché, squeezing out the salty sea water and making the paper small in her hand. She thinks about the lost person – a son perhaps, or a daughter; the photo has long since been torn away and swallowed by the sea. Sylvia has never had a child and she envies the French people their child at the same time as she deeply pities their loss. Until Roy came along, Sylvia had never loved anyone except Jeremy, although she had been loved and had run away from it because it crushed her.

'*Est-ce que vous avez vu cette personne?*' It strikes Sylvia that there's something pitifully inappropriate about the words that the sea nudges at her feet in this remote place. She never sees anyone except Roy, the elephant, the cow, the ducks, the chickens, the dog and the delivery man.

For the first time in a long while, Sylvia feels lonely as she goes to find the elephant and start the day's chores.

'Is it a bad omen if a magpie does a shit in someone's garden?' asks Alison.

'A lone magpie?' Taron turns to the window in alarm. 'Doing a shit in your garden?'

'I just wondered.' Alison watches Taron guiltily. She tries to discover from the look on her face whether Taron turned round quickly enough to see nature's black and white harbinger of ill fortune leaving its expressive message.

28

Cruising

Harvey joins the men's group held in one of the public meeting rooms available for hire in St Matthew's Church in Brixton. 'I think I need some help in coming to terms with identity,' Harvey told an acquaintance of his, a man he knows from the gym, someone he feels he has made a connection with as they chatted in the sauna or dried off in the shower area. 'I have this trouble with labels. It shouldn't matter but it does. Do you know what I mean?' The man, a little older than Harvey, with some hints of grey in his brown hair and soft, understanding green eyes, recommended Harvey check out the men's group that meets in Brixton on the first Tuesday of every month.

'We don't have a leader here,' says the leader of the group, a pleasant hint of a non-specific North American accent in his voice. 'We just use this as an opportunity to talk. This is a non-judgemental meeting. Jonathan, would you like to kick off tonight?'

Jonathan is a remarkably shy and inarticulate young man in his early twenties who grips the sides of his wooden chair as he talks. He looks as if he is testing its structural stability in case he wishes to straighten his arms and raise his body from the seat. Jonathan's contribution is difficult to follow, although he appears to be prefacing any salient comment he might be about to make with a long tribute to the group's role in helping him to face the difficulties of his life.

Harvey looks around the group. There is a nice mix of men, black and white, gay and straight. The gay ones have something of the look of his friend at the gym, their well-cared-for bodies giving them an indeterminate age anywhere between late thirties and middle forties. They all have a kindness in their faces and a comfortable-in-their-clothes (or out) attitude. The straight ones are all rather awkward-looking. Harvey has cruised the room with his eyes and made assumptions about sexual orientation based on two things: i) the gay ones have better grooming; ii) the gay ones have all cruised him back.

Jonathan has finished talking and has collapsed back into his seat, rubbing the palms of his hands on his trousers and blushing with the effort of expressing himself.

'Thank you, Jonathan,' says the leader. 'Mike, do you have a response to any of that?'

One of the gay men looks around the group and then addresses his remarks to Jonathan. 'The first thing is to love yourself, Jonathan. We love you.' There is muted applause. Harvey realizes the men in the group are not meeting for a philosophical discussion about how they perceive the world, but to discuss how to deal with the way the world perceives homosexual men.

Out and proud since he was about twelve, Harvey uses the distraction created by the applause to pick up his bag and head for the door. As he leaves, he glances back and makes eye contact with a tanned man with mesmerizing brown eyes and thick, cropped grey hair, so he will know him again if he sees him around.

29

High-Wire Workout

Roy is near the end of his daily high-wire preparation workout. He has been training himself to stand for lengthy periods on first one leg then the other, strengthening the muscles, and practising not falling over. Now he stands, feet placed hip distance apart, pointing forward, parallel to each other. The high-wire balance bar rests on the back of his neck, gripped in both hands. Slowly he squats, keeping his chin up and pushing his bottom out as he bends his knees. Then he rises back up again, slowly, repeating the movement about twenty times. Roy puts the balance bar slowly down on the ground, shaking his arms and legs, then starts to stretch every major muscle. The routine finished, Roy goes and lies on the top of a sand dune.

A light wind stirs the grass around him and tickles his face. He feels very warm from exercising. He remembers a children's TV programme he watched many afternoons ago during a tea break at the kennels. The presenter held two heavy weights in his hands for a full minute, then showed how his arms rose involuntarily when the weights were removed. Roy imagines every one of his aching muscles stretching upwards, lifting his body a few inches off the sand dune, high enough for the wind to reach underneath him and touch the flattened grass there. He breathes in slowly and deeply, pushing his stomach out to make room for the air in his lungs. As he breathes out, he feels that his body presses less heavily on the grass and sand. He feels that he is becoming light.

Sylvia watches out of the window for him. She looks down the path towards the vegetable patch where he tends and modifies his model of her house. She searches further, towards the end of her range of vision, and sees him lying on the sand dune. He looks abandoned, as if some other woman has finished playing with him and left him there to be picked up and brought home. He is so still that she wonders, just for a moment, whether he is alive. He is too far away for Sylvia to be able to detect the slow, deliberate rise and fall of his belly under his hands. Then she reminds herself that this is a place of safety, so far removed from the real world that nothing bad ever happens. She watches him get to his feet, dust himself off and make his way back towards the house.

That night, asleep on the white cotton sheets, Roy's arm around her, Sylvia dreams of her days in the circus. This dream starts, as it nearly always does, with her friend Pamela in an orange leotard, spinning plates.

Pamela, looking exactly as she did fifteen years ago, stands in the middle of the big top and stares directly at Sylvia. Plates spin on her foot, on her hands, on her forehead. Then the bendy acrobats in lemon body suits roll over and over in hoop shapes around her, their backs arched, heels touching their ears. Men in green sequins swing from trapezes. Children in red suits bounce above trampolines, then tumble back down again. Then the clowns come, big noses and big feet, pushing and shoving the others. Still Pamela stands in the middle, spinning plates, looking at Sylvia.

From the very top of the big top, from much higher up than

the point where Sylvia is looking in her dream, the daredevil acrobat starts to fall. His feet are tucked under his body, his hands grip his ankles. He turns over once in the air. He turns again. He will not be able to make another turn without smashing the plates, scattering the people. Sylvia wakes up before it happens. 'Jeremy,' she says. Two years ago, as soon as she learned it was wrong to put animals in the circus, she went to Jeremy and told him to leave, cutting him adrift from his life there. Now he falls from the roof of the big top in her dreams.

30

Frozen Yoghurt

Jane and Harvey have almost finished their lunch in Old Compton Street. Jane is on the dessert course, which Harvey has skipped. He stirs his double espresso languidly with a sugar-crystal stirrer while he waits for the coffee to cool.

'What is it that you see in Jeremy?' Harvey askes Jane. 'It can't just be the sex. You must know there will always be another man along if it doesn't work out.'

'It isn't just sex. It's his passion for the environment.'

'Oh, please.'

'It's true. Most people can't seem to get excited about anything but Jeremy cares about birdsong. I'd like to siphon off some of that passion for myself. And by the way, great sex isn't so easy to come by when you reach our age, Harvs, so even if it was only the sex, I'd stick with it for a while.'

'I dreamed last night that I was trying to give birth to a baby but it wouldn't come out,' Harvey tells Jane. 'What does that mean? And don't say it means I want to be a woman.'

'Obviously you don't want to be a woman, Harvs. It's terrible being a woman. I think it means you are trying to give birth to some creative project but it's blocked.'

'Maybe. Yes, that's very good. There is something.'

'What is it? Tell me what it is. I can try to midwife it.'

'I've been compiling my list identifying unnamed feelings. I've spent ages on it. It's a long list and it's starting to look quite comprehensive.'

'A long list? I wouldn't have thought you'd find that many. Why don't you tell me what you've got and we can try to double-check if they really are unnamed. I'll tell you if I can think of any word that matches the feeling.'

'Really, do you mind?'

'That's how scientists work. They test their theories before they publish them. We have to apply the same rigour to your wordless feelings. So what have you got?'

'Well, in the morning, the moment between dreams and sleep.'

'Waking up.'

'What?'

'That is called waking up. Next!'

'Jane.' Harvey folds his piece of paper. 'It's not funny.'

'Next!'

'You are the most irritating person I know.'

Jane is laughing so hard that the scoop of low-fat frozen raspberry yoghurt she has just put into her mouth starts to melt and she seems incapable of swallowing it without choking. Slow pink dribbles emerge from between her lips and run down her chin. A semi-solid dollop of yoghurt falls backwards off her spoon and makes a splash on her black trousers as she puts her hand to her mouth to wipe the yoghurt away. She tilts her face upwards and half opens her mouth, still laughing. Harvey sees a boiling cauldron of pink liquid in there, mixed by her tongue.

'Jane,' he hisses but this encourages her more. She makes a honking noise and sprays a fine pink mist over a wide area. As Harvey watches, a small spurt of yoghurt forces its way from each of Jane's nostrils and she wipes at her nose with the back of her hand.

Harvey walks away, leaving Jane bent over, elbows on the table, eyes shut against the tears, trying to catch her breath, still laughing helplessly. The maître d'raises his eyebrows very slightly at Harvey as an attractive waiter sashays to the table with a linen napkin to dab at his dishevelled lunch partner.

31

Laundry

In Paradise, Roy turns out his toes at a 45 degree angle, twisting his feet into the sand beneath the wiry grass near the sand dunes, like a ballroom dancer with a tray of talcum powder preparing a non-slip grip for the soles of his shoes. He remains where he is, leaning forward slightly into the wind. He brings up his arms, gracefully, until his elbows are level with his shoulders, relaxing his wrists so that his fingers hang downwards, casting feather-shaped shadows on the beach.

Roy is wearing Sylvia's shoes, which are size 8, and her clothes. In addition to her range of white and pink T-shirts and jeans, she has a selection of loose unisex and men's clothes: work shirts and sweat pants or combat trousers. He turns up the sleeves and belts the trousers in tight, the material hanging off his skinny bones. Once or twice he has wondered why she has a whole wardrobe full of men's clothes. Has she ever had another man here? He once asked her where she got the clothes and she shrugged and said, 'I've always had them.'

Leaning comfortably on the windowsill above the radiator in the kitchen, enjoying a mid-morning break, Sylvia watches him. Unaware, facing out towards the sea, he remains motionless for fifteen minutes until the weight of his own arms is uncomfortable and he drops them to his side, shaking his hands so that his fingers clack together. Seeing that he has finished, Sylvia draws herself up, wipes a heart in the mist where her breath has condensed on the window, and goes to switch on the kettle.

Sylvia, with her collection of elephant, dog, cow, ducks, chickens and Roy, who has fallen from the skies, thinks of herself as their protector. They have the freedom to wander anywhere on her property. They have food and water and somewhere comfortable out of the wind and rain and the sun. So long as she does not earn money from them, as a zoo keeper would, she feels she is doing the right thing by them. Any one of them is free to leave, although where would they go?

Too much attention suffocates Sylvia, she finds it intrusive. Living at Mrs Latimer's was comfortable at first but after a while she felt she couldn't breathe, as if she had her head in a feather pillow. Sylvia is scrupulous in attending to the needs of all her charges – she would never neglect them. But she likes to let them be, because that's how she likes to live.

Sheila is in her flat in Brixton, hemmed in by all the accumulated metal objects that she hopes will bring her news of Roy, her tinfoil receivers in place on her ears. She remembers the time, once before, when she thought she had lost him. He was nearly forty and he had been quieter than usual for a couple of weeks, taking stock of his life.

'I can't go on,' he said one day, coming into the kitchen. Sheila was crouched in front of the washing machine he had installed for her, sorting the clothes for a dark wash, pairing his vinegary socks before putting them into the washing drum so they would not get separated. Her hand rested on a thin pair of his boxer shorts, the cotton softened by too much wear. She had been thinking she would need to replace them for him soon.

'What do you mean?' She had been terrified. She had heard of women flying into a rage when a man threatened to end a relationship, throwing back all the things the man had ever given them. What had Roy given her? She'd be hard pressed to think of anything that wasn't bolted down except for a set of kitchen knives and a lampshade. His gifts to her were things that he constructed and nailed into place as if he thought, as she did, that there was no possibility of ever dismantling their home. There were the bookcases set into the recesses of the front room, shelves, cupboards, the fitted kitchen that he worked on all week while she holidayed in north Cornwall with her sister.

'I want to leave my job. I hate commuting in to the West End, taking orders from that lightweight who couldn't use a tape measure let alone a power drill but who has been given a managerial job because he can write reports. If I protect my pension I can retire early and we can live somewhere like Spain, where the cost of living is cheap and the climate is good. Until I retire I want something quieter, Sheila, where I am my own boss.' That was how he came to find the job at Mrs Latimer's.

Sheila had forgotten that unfounded fear of losing him, in the planning and the excitement surrounding his new job. When she has an intense memory of him, or some flash of an idea about where he might be, Sheila thinks of it as a message. What does this one mean? There is the remembered fear that he was going to leave her willingly; his wish for a quieter life; his love of building things around their home; the vivid picture of crouching in front of the washing machine and thinking that her life was going to change for ever. It could be a message about his laundry. He only has the clothes he disappeared in. Would the aliens have a washing machine? Have they perfected a kind of dry cleaning that allows Roy to remain fully clothed while they restore him to a pristine condition? Is he filthy and in rags? Is he naked, lying on a table with probes and scanners attached to his body while the aliens investigate his inner workings? The messages Sheila receives are becoming more intense but they are bewildering and upsetting. She finds that she is crying. It is unbearable to think that Roy is alone, without her there to help him. Sheila thought that she had no more tears to cry, but she does.

32

The Albert Memorial

It is Thursday night. Sheila has come alone to the Close Encounters meeting, where a discussion is underway about plans to visit the recently renovated Albert Memorial in Kensington Gardens to try to reach out to extraterrestrials.

'Why the Albert Memorial?' Sheila asks.

The members of the group are delighted with the question. They smile big, genuine smiles. 'You'll see, Sheila.'

'Is there any evidence that metal improves the reception of messages from aliens?' asks Sheila. The group is staring. 'I know metal is a conductor,' she continues hurriedly. 'I wondered if that had anything to do with it.'

'Have you had a message, Sheila?' Rosy asks her gently. She bends her head forward into the start of an encouraging nod and extends one hand towards Sheila, as if she is trying to entice a skittish animal to come closer. Everyone is still staring. Sheila is aware that they think she's weird. Weird, among a group of people who meet to discuss the best way of contacting aliens.

'Yes.'

Everyone is suddenly friendly. There are smiles all round. Friend catches the eye of friend. Enemy is reconciled to enemy. They all take one step forward, nearer to Sheila.

'My greatest success,' begins Sheila shyly, like a housewife describing her baking technique to a group of Michelin-starred chefs, 'has been with tinfoil.'

Roy has his hands in the sink, doing the washing up. It is late in the evening. He has the comfortable feeling that comes when it is nearly time for bed and he has been fed, and he has been out in the fresh air all day. There is a gentle 'tik, tik' sound of knitting needles as Sylvia scrapes them together, winding the wool round the needle in her right hand to form a neat stitch, flicking at the stitch with the needle in her left hand. Over and over, rhythmically. Sylvia has the yarn wound round the fingers of her right hand, her little finger extended as if she is a labourer drinking for the first time from a bone china cup in an audience with the Queen.

Roy dries his hands on a tea towel and turns to watch Sylvia. She is knitting a delicate pink garment on fine-gauge needles. The colour she has chosen would be suitable for a newborn baby girl but as the knitting grows too large for anything other than a giant's child, Roy sees that it must be something for Sylvia herself. She has a very faraway look in her eyes as she works carefully up and down the rows. If she makes a mistake, she painstakingly traces and re-works each dropped stitch as if it represents a mistake in the fabric of time.

Sylvia is thinking about Jeremy.

33

The Postman's Dog

The psychic postman has been sacked for over-sensitivity. If it was the post office's intention to improve the efficiency of the delivery service by doing this, their intention has backfired. Now Alison's post comes every two or three days, at some time between 1.00 p.m. and 2.30 p.m. The post is delivered in a bundle held together by an elastic band, some of it addressed to Alison but much of it addressed to other houses in the surrounding area. The bundling may be part of an unheralded post office initiative to promote neighbourliness. When the post arrives, Alison puts Phoebe in the stroller and spends the afternoon delivering it. She never sees any of her neighbours putting misdelivered post through her letterbox. Perhaps they open it up and keep it, their kitchen noticeboards plastered with poems from Jeff that were meant for her eyes.

'I got a note through my door from the post office this morning saying they tried to deliver a parcel,' Alison tells Harvey at the door to their house as she returns from one of her postal rounds. 'They didn't even ring the doorbell, so they didn't try very hard. It's so annoying. Why do they do that?'

'Most people round here are at work when the postman comes. Parcels are heavy and if they can't deliver them they have to carry them all the way back to the sorting office. They probably write the "can't deliver" notes before they set off and leave the parcels behind.'

'That's terrible.'

'It's what I'd do if I were a postman. If I get my camera will you come and take a photo of me in front of the new double billboard car advert that's gone up at Clapham Common? I wrote the copy for it.'

'What does it say?'

'Three little words. You'll have to wait and see. It's supposed to appeal to hetero men.'

'I hope they don't pay you by the word. No wonder you're so poor all the time.'

'It isn't the number of words. They pay me to deliver a concept. As you say, no wonder I'm so poor.'

As Harvey goes inside to retrieve his camera, the psychic postman arrives on Alison's doorstep with a crossbreed dog on a lead. The postman looks sheepish. The dog looks trusting and hungry. But then all dogs look hungry, in order to gain the sympathy of people with spare food. The postman hands over the lead to Alison. 'Will you take care of him for me? I'm going away to look for a job. I would take him to my parents' house in the West Country but a lot of the mink that were released by animal protesters are still on the loose. I'm worried that he would get attacked.'

The dog has fine, very fluffy fur on his paws that makes them look out of proportion to the rest of him, like a puppy who has yet to grow into his body.

'He looks like a teddy bear. What's his name?'

'Boy.'

The dog lies on the doormat and Alison strokes his ribs and belly.

'That's sweet. How old is he?'

'He's sixteen. He's an old man. He's completely deaf. In human years he's one hundred and two.'

Alison withdraws her hand, suddenly uncomfortable about stroking an old man's tender parts. The dog stands again with difficulty and Alison sees his age. A recent stroke has hitched the dog's face into a permanent Roger Moore impression. The smell of smoky bacon that emanates from him, far from being off-putting, is making Alison rather hungry.

'Come on, Boy. Boy. BOY,' shouts Alison. As she takes him inside to get used to his temporary home, Boy leaves a trail of silky fur. Phoebe follows unsteadily behind him, swiping at his tail.

'This?' asks Phoebe, pointing to the dog.

'There's enough here to weave you a jacket,' Alison tells Phoebe as she collects the fur from the carpet. 'They should have called him Rumpelstiltskin.'

'Alison.' Mrs Fitzgerald is on the phone. 'How are you doing for money, my dear?'

'Not very well.'

'I thought you might be struggling with that wee baby to support. You haven't been working much lately. I've got a nice job for you with a big bonus at the end of it. You have to find a missing person but it should be easy enough. I've got some ideas about how you can find her. In fact I've already started making some inquiries. All you have to do is have sight of her, make sure she's the right person, bash out a quick five-hundred-word health, wealth and happiness report and the fee and the bonus are yours. I should warn you that I have accepted the assignment on your behalf with some misgivings.'

'What misgivings?'

'There are some elements of Mrs Latimer's operation that I must turn over to be investigated by the police. Do you have a moment to talk about it? She says she wants to breed men as pets.'

'That's insane.'

'Yes. I have an old friend from the Met. Let me talk to him and find out how to handle this. In the meantime, I suggest you find this missing person quickly and earn yourself some money, before Mrs Latimer gets herself arrested.'

Alison thinks as she puts down the phone, as she always does when she talks to Mrs Fitzgerald, that her boss is wise and kind. There is something else that Alison picked up in the tone of her voice today, some lightness in her mood that hasn't been there before.

'I am not mad,' Mrs Fitzgerald is thinking, the phone still in her hand. 'I have stared into the face of publicity-seeking Venetia Latimer and I have seen madness. I am not mad. If I continue to avoid any kind of publicity I will be safe.'

Jeremy's hands are very tanned. Deep in thought, he traces his forefinger over the architectural drawings. The fine hairs on his arm catch sunlight with the movement. He looks up at his friends, watching him silently.

'This will be the performance of a lifetime. We'll be creating art, we'll be making a political protest, we'll be investing in the future of the planet.'

'Couldn't we do something at the Millennium Dome? We could paint a message there so it could be seen from space.'

'Why? No one will see it except a handful of astronauts. Everyone is trying to stage a protest at the Dome. Besides, there are circus performers there as part of the exhibition. It wouldn't be much of a protest if we got mixed up with them. My plan is much better. We're going to hold to ransom one of the most easily recognizable images in the world.'

'Will we wear black? Black clothes and balaclavas?'

'No. Let's dress up in our brightest costumes. It's gonna be the biggest circus in town.'

'Yeah, we're celebrating.'

'Yeah, we're gonna stop the traffic. Listen, I'm serious now, the only thing that matters more than looking good for the performance is our personal safety. I'll climb to the top first, then I'll run lines down for the rest of you. Not one of you climbs until your line is secure, understood?

'When are we going to do it?'

'Soon. Before the end of July. The light at the top of the tower only shines at night when the Commons is sitting so we have to strike before their summer recess, to ensure we can see what we're doing. I think we also need to choose a night when the moon is full so visibility will be even better.'

The meeting disbands and Jeremy is left alone with Jane. Jane sometimes finds Jeremy's naivety irritating. He is always protesting about something, either standing in the road in everyone's way or making nuisance phone calls. His head is so filled with principles that he doesn't even seem interested in her. No wonder he drips with pheromones, his sexuality leaking out through his pores as it has no other outlet.

Jeremy is pulling at a locket on a chain round his neck, sawing it left and right, left and right. It looks like the kind of medallion with a picture of a saint on it that a religious or southern European person would wear. Jane is very tall. She stands face to face with Jeremy, very close, as she prises open the locket and inspects the faded photo of Sylvia glued inside it.

'My sister. She's the one who made me leave the circus. She's spent her life savings on a rundown farm. She said it will come to me when she dies but it doesn't really compensate for the loss of a life that I loved. Sometimes I wish I hadn't left the circus.'

'What if you die first?'

'Why should I die?'

'Because you take risks. You lost your security when you were young. No wonder you're trying to control something as impossible as the traffic. You may as well try and command the waves.' When Jane gains some kind of insight into other people's psychological motivations, it always puts her in a better mood.

'Alison? It's Sheila. I've had another message. It came to me while I was reading this report in the paper that Rosy gave to me. Listen to this: "Dolphins have been sighted up and down one of the most unspoiled stretches of the south coast of England for the first time in fifty years, taking advantage of the unseasonal warmth of the seas caused by the recent hot weather." The dolphins have been coming right up to the shore and playing. I'd like to make my picture of Roy somewhere on that coastline. Rosy says that it will be the perfect location to try and get in touch with extraterrestrials, with the dolphins nearby to help us.'

'Well, I've got to head off in that direction some time soon anyway, on a missing elephant inquiry. I can take you with me, if you like. I'll bring my daughter if I can't get a babysitter, if you don't mind. When were you thinking of going?'

'When there's a full moon because the tides are high and also there will be plenty of light on the picture at night so it can be seen from the sky.'

'Don't they have those very powerful beams of light from spaceships? I wouldn't think it would make much difference whether there was a full moon or not for people in, um, interplanetary craft. I take your point about the high tides, though. I suppose it will enable the dolphins to float closer in to the shore.'

34

The Bridges

Jane Memory is on the phone to a features editor. Whenever Jane telephone this editor from her house, he always has the impression that she's doing something else while she's talking to him. He pulls at the hairs on his leg just above the line of his sock and visualizes her depilating her legs in the bathroom, ladling on hot wax with a spatula.

'I want to write about people who are yummy and attractive on the outside but who are empty inside.' Jane is lying on her bedroom floor, a blue and green checked pillow under her head. The editor imagines her leaning forward at her bathroom mirror, tweezering away stray eyebrow hairs. 'What do you think? The research would be easy. I've got a friend chasing all over town looking for something to give his life meaning so I could write that up, thinly disguised. It would be quite amusing.'

'I was hoping to get you to do us an evaluation of the first salon in London to offer a Brazilian bikini wax.'

'Is that where they pull all the hairs out of your bum?'

'Every last one, apparently.'

'Let me write my piece about empty people and I'll do it.'

'We are on a suicide watch,' announces Taron.

'Are we?' Joey and Hugo are dressed for the pub.

'I'm worried about this man who's going to jump off a bridge into the Thames. We have to go and stop him.'

'OK. Which bridge is he on?' Hugo jingles his car keys in his trouser pocket, ready for action. He was in the rugby team at school and has lost none of his strength or speed.

'That's just it. I don't know. It's a vision my mother keeps having. If we patrol the bridges we're bound to find him.'

In practice, the three don't patrol all the bridges, just the more scenic and convenient ones. They like Waterloo Bridge because it leads directly to the South Bank with its choice of coffee shops and clean toilets among the complex of theatres and recital halls. They become a familiar sight to the beggars lining the footbridge, who say nothing and look preoccupied when they pass, having learnt that Taron prefers to dispense advice rather than cash.

'We three work,' says Taron, plucking a pound coin from Hugo's fingers as he crosses to a youth in a sleeping bag and thrusting it deeply and intimately back into Hugo's pocket. 'There is no point sharing the profits from it. We should share the insights. If you belonged to a really cool drinking club, would your friends thank you for smuggling out some of the Japanese rice crackers that had been put out on the bar, or would they prefer you to tell them how to get in and snack for free for themselves?'

'But the money markets?'

'It's about empowerment. I'm not saying they should sit at a desk across from you at the bank. They need to know how to tap into their talents and get some money and some self-respect.'

'A spell in the army might sort them out,' says Joey, laughing nervously and winking at Hugo, who is trying to mouth 'fascist' without Taron seeing.

There is no sign of anyone trying to jump. When the drizzle of passers-by stops altogether in the evenings, they catch a cab to Chelsea Bridge. Taron looks west along the Thames while Joey and Hugo look east. While Taron is turned away, Joey and Hugo like to play 'Titanic', climbing on to a parapet along the structure of the bridge and taking it in turns to be Kate Winslett.

'I've got a bit of a strange request, Taron,' Joey says one night. 'My mother needs to get hold of twenty grammes of speed. Do you know where she could get it?'

'I'm sorry, Joey, I've given up doing drugs. I'm just living on my memories.'

'Yes, but do you know where I could get hold of it? If she can't have speed, she said she'll take thirty or forty tabs of LSD. She just wants something cheap, she's not bothered about the effects.'

'Joey, have you thought this through? Why are you doing this?'

'Because she asked me to.'

'Wouldn't it be simpler just to tell her about Hugo, rather than trying to do everything she asks as a way of storing up her approval?'

'It isn't like that.'

'When there is something that is worrying you, you should write it on a small piece of paper, fold the paper and put it in a matchbox on a piece of cotton wool, as if you were making a bed for a doll. Then throw it into the Thames and watch it float away.'

'Do you think your mother is wrong?' Joey asks Taron after a week. He knows there is something troubling her because when he was supposed to be watching the river he saw her casting a matchbox into the river from Westminster Bridge. 'We've spent every night looking and we haven't seen one person who has given any indication that they are going to jump.'

'No. Maybe. But maybe we've been sending out such good energy that we've diverted someone from feeling like jumping. At any rate, I think we've earned ourselves a holiday, don't you?'

'Yes,' says Hugo. He jumps up and swings on every lamppost on the short walk to the nearest late-night bar.

35

The Circus

'Why are you here?' the clairvoyant asks.

'I was hoping you could tell me that,' Harvey replies, casting an eye around the flat in Josephine Avenue. The decoration is a little tired. 'I'm constantly afraid. I feel that I'm missing out on something but I don't know what. I don't know how to tackle it.'

'There is a cause that you should champion.' The clairvoyant holds her hand up, palm forward, as if to signify a Native American peace greeting. Harvey takes it as an instruction not to speak. 'I can't tell you what it is. Once you identify it, you will find fulfilment.'

Her advice is of very little use, so far as Harvey can see. And the woman has a cat. Luckily he took the precaution of swallowing an antihistamine tablet before he came out. Why is it that mystic types always keep animals? The fabric of her blouse pulls slightly at the buttons. Harvey can see Dorothy's freckled flesh in the gaps she makes in her clothing when she moves. He fixes his eye on the Lladro duck on her mantelpiece until it is time to leave.

'One more thing. I can see a man falling from somewhere

very high up. I'm not sure when it will happen but it is an event that is going to change your life.'

A little top has appeared on Clapham Common. A little top is like a big top in every respect except size. A line drawing of an acrobat advertises a one-man show on red and white posters pasted on local telegraph poles. A poorly drawn moustache garnishes many of the posters, courtesy of an anonymous local graffiti artist.

Venetia Latimer sits on the hard bench in the little top in her finery and thinks about Sylvia. She thinks about the way Sylvia looks when she washes her hair in the bath. Her face, naked without make-up, tilted upwards against the spray of the showerhead, her eyes closed to keep the water out. The freckles visible on Sylvia's nose and across her cheeks under long brown eyelashes pressed together in a semi-circle, catching drops of water on their ends. Pale eyebrows, pink lips, white teeth, unlined skin. Sylvia looks younger than her thirty-nine years. Mrs Latimer is remembering her the way she was thirty-one when she first came to live in her house.

The water swells and dulls Sylvia's bright yellow hair and makes it look soft and greyish, like wet feathers. Venetia removes the shower attachment from its hook on the wall above the bath and takes it in her right hand. The nubs of the individual vertebrae are visible through Sylvia's skin as she leans forward, her knees drawn up, her spine curving slightly, while Venetia directs the shower away from her towards the back of the bath, adjusting the temperature, darting her left hand back and forth into the water to test it.

Venetia takes her left hand and puts it flat against Syliva's forehead where her hairline begins, then makes a curve with her hand and presses it hard to fit against the curve of Sylvia's head, following her hand with the spray of water. When she reaches the ends of Sylvia's hair she squeezes it gently. She repeats this process several times until the shampoo is rinsed away completely and the water coming from Sylvia's hair runs clear. Then Venetia brings her hand to the top of Sylvia's head once more and digs her fingers in through her hair, massaging her scalp.

At first when she helped Sylvia wash her hair, Venetia used to kneel at the side of the bath but the effort made her breathe heavily and her weight on her knees made them uncomfortable. One day she found a three-legged milking stool in a bric-a-brac store in the village and that made the task much easier.

When she looked at Sylvia in the bath, pink nipples resting on the shelf of white skin where her stomach jutted outwards from her belly button, Venetia used to think that Sylvia looked as if she had been packed for a long journey by a thoughtful god or other supreme being. She had spares of everything. As she sat sideways on, facing the taps, the roll of fat under her bosoms looked like a shadow set, in case the first should go missing. When Sylvia stood in the bath, before she bent to pull the plug, Venetia could see scoops of fat at the tops of Sylvia's thighs which, with her buttocks, make a shape like butterfly wings.

Finally Sylvia would turn and shake the water from her body before stepping into the embrace of the extra large white bath towel that Venetia held up for her, clean and warm from the airing cupboard.

Venetia Latimer opens her eyes and stops remembering just as the audience breaks into applause for the circus performer in the little top in front of her.

Venetia wanted to feel closer to the circus, by being close to Sylvia. Sylvia was easy to confide in because she absorbed everything, apparently without judgement, and told nothing in return. Venetia gave away so much of herself to Sylvia, hoping to plant some part of herself in Sylvia and make it grow, as if they were living in a less educated era when women, even married women like Venetia, were rather vague about where babies come from. She used to watch Sylvia with pride, fat and gettting fatter, walking around her house apparently swollen from all the love and attention she received from her mentor, as if she really might give birth at any minute to a miraculous circus child engendered by love alone.

The next day is the anniversary of the first visit to London of animal trainer Rudolph Knie. An advertisement appears in the personal column of *The Times* newspaper.

'It doesn't matter about the elephant. Please come back. V.'

36

Prince Albert

Sheila meets up with other members of the Close Encounters Group at the Albert Memorial in Kensington Gardens. She sets off at dusk in the pouring rain. It is an easy journey to Kensington Gardens from Brixton. Sheila could have taken the Victoria Line, which is modern, clean, quick and efficient, changed on to the District Line (which is not) and stepped off the Tube at South Kensington. She has chosen to drive. There are plenty of parking spaces on Exhibition Road next to Imperial College, its windows giving a view to basements filled with heavy machinery, work benches, pulleys, metal tubing the diameter of a man's height, all assembled to study and measure invisible things, like pressure and temperature and sound waves.

Sheila walks up the steps to Kensington Gardens from the pedestrian crossing in Kensington Gore and meets the other members of the encounter group on the chequered stones, black, brown and white, in front of the Albert Memorial. The ground is freshly wet but it has stopped raining and the sky is clear.

In 1868 the architect Sir George Gilbert Scott, inspired by the shrines of medieval times, designed an ornate memorial to Queen Victoria's husband Albert, prematurely dead at forty-two in 1861 and sadly mourned by the Queen until her own death in 1901.

The figures of Dante, Homer, Shakespeare, Goethe gather at the memorial. The assembled poets, artists and scientists create a testament to achievement that must impress anyone who sees it, even beings from other worlds, no matter how advanced the culture they hail from. Pink granite and red granite were brought from Scotland for the pillars and the pedestal; grey granite from Ireland for four pillars made from single stones each weighing 17 tons; Portland stone for the arches of the canopy and semi-precious stones in the mosaic.

I must find him, thinks Sheila, walking around the memorial to study the statues of the four continents. She remembers an old skipping song she and her friends used to sing in primary school:

North, South, East, West
Find the boy that I like best.

The Albert Memorial, 175 feet tall, is stunningly, goldenly, symmetrically beautiful. Golden stars shine in a blue mosaic canopy above where Albert sits, one knee raised, a programme for the Great Exhibition in his hand. Golden angels are above him, the monument topped with a golden cross. The marble frieze of poets, scientists and other notables is below him. In all, 169 figures crowd the monument. The marble figures at the four corners of the monument depicting the four continents shine brilliantly white. Albert himself is newly dipped in gold following the recent ten-million-pound restoration project. 'For a life devoted to the public good' reads part of the inscription in the canopy above him.

If a monument were to be built to commemorate Roy's life, what would it say? Is it possible to define your life with great works, for example as the prime mover behind the Great

Exhibition, as Albert was? The Crystal Palace that housed the exhibition, visited by six million people, was built in Hyde Park in just six months using more than 290,000 panes of glass. Can a person expect redemption through one great act or is it necessary to live well all your life?

Prince Albert was forty-two when he died, probably from typhoid. Roy's age. It is uncanny, Roy and Sheila and Queen Victoria and Prince Albert all being the same age. It is like being thrown together with another couple in a queue for Wimbledon or waiting to see Princess Diana's funeral procession and discovering they have so much in common. If they had met at a caravan park in North Wales during two weeks in August they would say 'we must keep in touch', but the contact has been made through a historical monument, across a time span of over a hundred years. It is more than a chance encounter. It is another message. The tinfoil is working. Roy Travers has disappeared from Brixton but his life is not over yet. Sheila may be forty-two but she feels as young and vigorous as she did on her twenty-first birthday. She will get Roy back if she has to fight for the rest of her life to set him free.

Sheila turns round from the Albert Memorial to face the Royal Albert Hall. She makes a little 'Oh' sound at the familiar sight of the enormous oval red-brick building, with its glass domed ceiling. She sees clearly as she never has before that it is modelled on the shape of a spaceship. 'You see, Sheila?' members of the group ask her. It is a beautiful moment for all of them.

'This hall was erected for the advancement of the Arts and Sciences and Works of Industry of all Nations' proclaims the inscription running round the Royal Albert Hall. Albert bought the site with proceeds from the £186,000 profit he made from the Great Exhibition in 1851. Even with the predicted crash in house prices, that sum is unlikely to buy more than a one-bedroom second-floor flat in Clapham these days. The Victorians experienced some delay in raising the funds to build on the site. The foundation stone was laid by Queen Victoria in 1867 and the hall was finished in 1871, when it was inaugurated by the Bishop of London and the unfortunate echo was first noticed.

It is raining again. The rain is running down Sheila's sleeve and soaking her blouse. As the near relative of someone who has been captured by aliens, Sheila enjoys an elevated status among the encounter group. Nevertheless, there has been some jealousy over Sheila's tinfoil ear caps. One or two of the members have taken to wearing tinfoil to meetings, although they are cagey about whether or not this has heightened their sensitivity to messages from extraterrestrials.

The boy who wears Adidas insists on sharing Sheila's umbrella as he hasn't brought one of his own, but there isn't enough room for the two of them to shelter under it. He is wearing a home-made tinfoil skull cap under a woollen Quicksilver beenie hat popular with snowboarders and other adventurous yet fashionable young people.

Rosy draws Sheila aside to talk about dolphins again. This time there is a greater note of anxiety in her voice. 'Did you read today's papers?' she asks Sheila. 'A dozen dolphins were washed up from the Pacific Ocean with small puncture holes in their skin, as if something had been implanted in them and then detonated. The reporter says they had been trained to detect mines as part of a French military experiment and then blown up when the experiment concluded.'

'Really? That's horrible.'

'It's nonsense. It's obvious they were assassinated by the CIA because they had been making contact with extraterrestrials. You mustn't waste any time in getting to the Kent coast to make your picture, Sheila, before the dolphins there meet a similar fate.'

As Sheila engages in a polite tugging match over the umbrella with the Adidas boy, she looks up and sees a bright ellipse-shaped light in the sky. The edge of the umbrella moves where it is pulled, providing greater shelter for her companion, and blocking out Sheila's view of the light in the sky. By the time she pulls the umbrella back again and looks up, the light has gone, hidden behind a cloud. The few seconds' sight of the spaceship are enough. It is another sign. Sheila makes up her mind to go to the coast within the next few days.

37

The Smallest Room

Jane telephones Harvey from 'the smallest room in her house' as her mother used to call it. It is neat and tidy, decorated in dark blue with a marine motif. Jane's bathroom has none of the range of feminine hygiene products showily displayed by other women of her age in their homes. Jane simply has no need to let visitors know that she menstruates. Her moods usually advertise the progress of her monthly cycles adequately enough.

'Can you come to Westminster with me tomorrow to do some filming? Jeremy is going to the top of Big Ben to see how to stop it and I want to get some pictures.'

'Why does he want to stop it?'

'It's part of a protest, he wants to turn back time.'

'Like Tina Turner?'

'No, like Cher. He wants to go up there tomorrow to see whether we need any specialist equipment on the big day,'

'Like blowtorches, you mean? Or a spanner? Is there a spanner big enough to unscrew the nuts and bolts that hold the hands on the clock faces?'

'I mean harnesses, specialist equipment for the performance. He hopes that if three of them hang off each end of the minute hands at the same time they can jam the mechanism.'

'I heard they balance the mechanism with old pennies. In fact I think I saw it on *Blue Peter* once. If you just collect all the old pennies in the land and wait for the ones they use to wear out then it will go haywire eventually. It would be rather sweet, like collecting all the needles so Sleeping Beauty wouldn't prick herself.'

'There would be a national appeal for old pennies funded by the *Sun* newspaper and broadcast on *Crimewatch* and someone would find a store of them under a pensioner's bed. Anyway, hiding pennies and waiting for something to go wrong isn't very visual. I want you to come with me to see whether you can film from Parliament Square or whether we need to get inside the car park in the House of Commons and set up the camera on St Stephen's Green.'

'Is that the bit of grass where politicians are interviewed for the evening news?'

'Yes. The police won't let us into the grounds unless we have a valid reason to be there. I might be able to swing an invite with my press pass, although I wouldn't want Jeremy's antics linked back to me, it might destroy my career. It would help if we knew an MP. Do you know any of the gay ones, Harvs?'

'Because I'm gay, do you mean?'

'Yes.'

'No, I don't.'

'It's got to look great and I have to be sure we can capture everything on camera. It's a full moon tomorrow night and the weather forecast is fine for a change so we should have a clear view. The whole group is going to attempt the protest at the next full moon so we'll have four weeks to iron out any problems but on the night itself we won't have much time for fancy camerawork. While Jeremy's on his own up there tomorrow I'd like to try and get some shots we can cut into the film we shoot next month. I want him silhouetted in black as he passes across the clock face, flying like Peter Pan.'

'I went to see one of those yogic flying gurus at the Royal Albert Hall on Saturday. I didn't go in because it was too crowded but I got talking to a very interesting woman outside, all patchouli oil, hair extensions and henna tattoos. I told her about naming things and she said that my search for the truth is external and that instead I should look inside myself.'

'Nonsense, you are looking inside yourself for the answers, that's just the problem. You're afraid of everything because there has never been any one thing that you have had to worry about. You need to find something, some cause that can test your limits and you need to fight for it to take your focus outside yourself.'

'This isn't a Foreign Legion thing, is it? I don't think you can join the military over twenty-six and I never got further than O-level French.'

'Don't be flippant, Harvey. That's what comes of taking advice from hippies. I doubt she could even find her way to the service station to buy chocolate to cure the munchies, let alone signpost the way towards the Great Truth for you. What do you really care about? If you don't know, then find something. Your whole life should be an act of defiance, then you wouldn't be afraid.'

'So it doesn't matter about naming things? Are you saying I've been going down the wrong track and I should live life as some kind of performance art? Do you live like that?'

'No, but I don't have to. I was reading about it in Waterstone's the other day while Philippe was buying some artsy film book. We all have different roles and we have to identify and accept them. All that caveman hunter-gatherer thing is bollocks. We're civilized now. This is Cool Britannia. We're starting the new renaissance and we have to learn from the models of old renaissance societies. Find what you're good at, or what you want to be good at. It doesn't really matter, so long as you do it for the greater good. For example, I should be a poet and you should be a knight. There were some other roles, I think, like the princess in the tower and the evil witch, the monk and the wandering jester, but I didn't read about them because they didn't sound very relevant so we'll have to make do with the poet and the knight. The poet is the chronicler, the knight is the crusader. I'm OK because I earn my living by writing but you've never had a fight in your life.'

'Are you saying that I needn't have embarked on this long search to confront my fears, I could have just browsed through a self-help book in a bookshop?'

'Yes.'

'I should live valiantly?'

'Yes.'

'Damn.'

38

Big Ben

Alison has been too preoccupied with the postman's dog and the baby to photograph Harvey's new advert. Before committing to be involved in tonight's filming, Harvey has persuaded Jane to follow him around south and west London with his stills camera. Jane has taken Harvey's photograph from several angles in front of the giant hoardings in Vauxhall, Hammersmith and Clapham Common that bear the latest car advert with Harvey's strapline: 'To Die For'.

When they get to Westminster that night, Jane and Harvey set up their camera on the grass on the Parliament Square roundabout, just next to the statue of Churchill looking uncomfortable in an overcoat and listing slightly to his right. Jeremy is already there. He is wearing peacock blue and seville orange Lycra, trimmed with velvet and accessorized with matching tights.

'You look like a harlequin Hamlet,' Jane tells him, checking her watch. It is midnight. Even though there is a full moon tonight, the opulence of his outfit would be lost in the darkness if it weren't for the bright lights Jane has borrowed from Philippe to illuminate Jeremy's ascent of the clock tower.

He straps a belt round his waist. Each of twelve pockets sewn into the belt contains a dummy hand grenade.

'No,' says Jane, stepping forward to unbuckle the belt and remove it. 'You look like as if you're wearing one of those flotation devices that toddlers use when they're learning to swim. Ready, Harvs? Action.'

'I'm going to stop the traffic,' says Jeremy, direct to the camera lens, a little loudly because he is wearing earplugs against the sound of the bells.

'Oh my God,' says Harvey, his voice very small, his face unseen behind the camera.

'If anything happens to me, if I get arrested or die in the attempt, will you take this locket and find Sylvia? I want you to tell her she's wrong. She mustn't fight against the circus.'

Jane pokes Harvey with a Biro under the ribs to make sure he's still filming. She puts out her hand and takes Sylvia's address that Jeremy is holding, written on a folded piece of paper, and she takes the locket. It is small enough to lie in the palm of her hand, in the hollow bordered by the deep creases that form her heart line and her life line.

When the bells have finished chiming midnight, Jeremy starts to climb to the top of Big Ben, dragging ropes and harnesses with him so he can fix them on the tower. This is a job usually undertaken by rigging experts. Jeremy is a performer.

By twenty past midnight he has reached the spire. By a quarter to one he has fixed the apparatus.

'Come on,' says Jane, jiggling about on the spot like a little girl needing to use the toilet.

Jeremy grasps the end of a thick rope, two inches in diameter and sealed with wax at its end. He tugs at the rope to engage the pulley system, then jumps into nothing so he can make a quick descent to reach the first set of clock hands, flying more like Errol Flynn than Peter Pan. The pulley fails to engage and he falls ten or fifteen feet very fast then stops. He hangs awkwardly for a few seconds as if the rope is caught or he has managed to catch hold of something to stop his fall. Then he falls again, reaching the ground very quickly, landing near the mini traffic lights by the car search area in front of the Houses of Parliament.

Jane and Harvey run across the road into Bridge Street and peer through the railings. It is plain to see Jeremy is dead, lying pale and smashed on the ground like a hard-boiled egg taken from a schoolboy's pocket. It is a few minutes before one o'clock.

Harvey is still filming. Jane turns to do a piece to camera, white-faced and shocked. She pauses, unable to find the right words. 'Oh my God,' she says. With her silver-ringed right hand, she covers her mouth and the whole lower half of her face, from nose to chin.

Harvey and Jane talk all night. Jeremy's death is very shocking to them, even for two such sophisticated city-dwellers. When they talk about things that trouble them, usually, it is in the hope of rationalizing their feelings and even achieving some kind of a consensus that they can live with. This approach doesn't seem to be working tonight.

'I had started to feel that it was within my power to make Jeremy happy or not happy,' Jane tells Harvey. 'Do you think that means I was in love with him?'

'Maybe he was in love with you, which is even worse, because you end up feeling responsible for someone if they are in love with you.'

'Well, you know, I'd been wondering what was going on because I've never been in love before. I didn't even wonder about whether he was in love with me. I knew he loved Sylvia. He mentioned Sylvia a few times.'

'Did I tell you he rang me up once, ages ago? All this time you were talking about Jeremy and sex and birdsong and climbing Big Ben and I didn't realize that he was the one who called me up about stopping the traffic. I'd often wondered what he was like and what he was doing. I never thought he'd be like that. I never thought I'd watch him die.'

'Who would ever think that?'

'Do you think that if I'd managed to make some kind of connection with him then, things would have turned out differently?'

'Harvey, don't.'

'Do you think that he jumped?'

'Don't.'

'Do you think that it would be better if he'd jumped, and he was trying to do one wild, brave thing and he threw his life away for it? Or would it be better if he'd slipped?'

'I don't think anything. I feel numb. I suppose we have to go and tell Sylvia.'

39

Philippe Starck

'I don't know if I belong here,' Roy tells Sylvia. His muscles ache from his recent preparations for the high wire.

'If you let go of your past life it will be easier, Roy,' Sylvia tells him. She says the words that give her comfort sometimes. 'Only believe.'

'I usually plan my wedding when I'm alone on long journeys,' Alison tells Sheila. Sitting next to Alison in the front of the car, her limp red hair a few points brighter than Alison's in nature's colour spectrum, Sheila could be a close relative rather than a client. She has left behind the tinfoil ear muffs that she habitually wears and looks the part of a respectable, ordinary woman on an outing.

'I didn't know you were getting married.' Sheila rallies at this piece of good news from her friend.

'I'm not. That's why it passes the time so well – I can linger over every lavish detail because there's no need to ground the planning in any kind of reality. I don't think I'll ever get married again.'

'Haven't you got a boyfriend?'

'No. I don't really want one. I know I shut myself off from people too much but I think they always betray you in the end.'

'That's awfully cynical.'

'I hate the way men can finish one relationship and pick up where they left off with the next one. They're like ruminants, wandering from one field of grass to the next, hardly lifting their heads up from grazing to notice what's going on around them.'

'Women are like that too, sometimes. You just haven't found the right man. That's why I think so much of Roy. He isn't like that.'

'Yes, you could be right. There is someone who cares about me. He sent me some lip gloss. I might give him a call when we get to the coast, after I've wrapped up this missing person inquiry.'

'As soon as I met him I thought Roy and I would always be together. It was quite easy to see the old man in him, to see how we'd grow old together, nipping the edges of a tidy lawn in the summer, building a fire in the living-room grate in the winter. I thought I was investing in a certainty.' Sheila, talking of Roy as if he were the South Sea Bubble, slips a metal colander on her head. The conical shape of the Philippe Starck design fits her quite snugly.

'That's an expensive-looking colander, Sheila.'

'If I used a cheap one with the traditional round shape it would slip about every time I move my head, besides looking like a World War One tin helmet.'

'Oof. You wouldn't want that.' Alison is very cheerful, looking forward to the drive.

Sheila is also looking forward to reaching the coast. She has packed a large, folded piece of paper with a grid pencilled on it. The contours of Roy's face are plotted on the grid with Xs.

A young police constable arrives at Mrs Latimer's house. If Mrs

Latimer didn't have her office at home, she would rarely have to open the door or answer the telephone herself. If she worked for a large organization there would be a receptionist or a personal secretary to do it for her. Her secretary is a local woman from the village and she only works in the mornings. It is already lunchtime and Mrs Latimer is eating a goat's cheese tartlet with new potato salad. The secretary has gone home to feed her children, and all the silly boys who work for Mrs Latimer are taking a break somewhere, eating their sandwiches in the fields or smoking dope. Mrs Latimer goes to the door, still carrying her fork somewhat absent-mindedly. She will remember the fork when she looks back on this moment.

'I wonder if you can help me,' the constable begins. 'A young man has been involved in an accident. I'm trying to trace his next of kin.'

'Oh, my God. Not Joey? Is it Joey?'

'No. The young man's name is Jeremy.'

'Oh, then you're looking for Sylvia.'

'I'm sorry, madam, I didn't mean to worry you. Is she here?'

'No.'

'We'll try her at her other address, in Kent. Is she there, do you think?'

'Let me just,' Mrs Latimer grabs for the constable's notebook, 'have a look. Yes, yes, down by the coast. Is Jeremy all right?'

'I really need to inform the next of kin, madam, before I can tell you that.'

'Oh my God, is he dead then?' Mrs Latimer shuts the door, gesturing with the fork so that the constable will leave before she forgets Sylvia's address. She rushes to the message pad by the telephone in the hallway and writes down Sylvia's address, then she sits in the chair by the phone and she puts her face in her hands and she cries. Emotion overtakes her.

She tries to deal with the awful, horrible fear that she felt even for a few seconds when she thought she had lost Joey; with relief that he is alive; with the longed-for possibility of finding and reuniting with Sylvia. The contrasting emotions following so quickly on the richness of the goat's cheese make her feel nauseous. She remains in the shadows in the hallway for a little while, recovering.

Venetia goes to sit at the antique cherrywood desk that once belonged to her mother-in-law. Inside the top drawer there lies the one remaining secret that Venetia Latimer felt she must share with Sylvia, years ago, when she still lived here. She had told all her business secrets. She had explained her cash flow projections and her profit margins, she had shown her the suitcase of money she kept in the safe for emergencies. She had led Sylvia by the neck into the ring, so she could interpret the performance from a dog's perspective. She helped Sylvia understand the best way to care for the elephant she had given her. Venetia had given her a lot but she wanted to give more. She runs over the incident in her mind. Again.

'We must not just share the good times,' Venetia tells Sylvia. The moment has come to show Sylvia her terrible burden and ask her to share it. She takes Sylvia into the office. The expensive furniture throws shadows in the room; the writing bureau, every occasional table and every chair an emblem of the money that flowed into the house when Venetia's trust fund was united with Stephen's.

Black and white photographs in silver frames document some of Venetia's recent achievements. She shakes hands heartily with Prince Charles at Highgrove House during a high point in her career in the mid-eighties. She caresses her favourite Dalmation on a sentimental afternoon in the early nineties. A space opposite the doorway has been reserved for future triumphs and will one day be occupied by the photographic portrait of her, 2 feet wide and 3 feet high, taken to illustrate Jane Memory's article on successful business women.

Venetia takes Mrs Fitzgerald's report on cruelty to animals and lays it in Sylvia's hands. 'This is what we are up against.' Sylvia looks at Venetia in that slow way of hers, takes the report and reads it there in the office, sitting on a re-upholstered chair reserved for visitors, her foot wound round one of the Queen Anne legs.

Venetia said 'we' because she meant to show Sylvia that they were equals at last and that she had shared everything with her, there was nothing else left to give. She wanted Sylvia to know that she loved her and to love her back. Those were to be the last words she ever said to Sylvia. She had heard voices raised in anger when Jeremy came to visit unexpectedly late that night but she hadn't interfered, thinking Sylvia was shrugging off her old life. By the next morning Sylvia was gone.

In Paradise, Sylvia is thinking of Jeremy, whom she loves. She does not yet know he is dead. Two years ago, Venetia Latimer gave Sylvia a report to read entitled 'Unkindness Kills' and then, smack, Sylvia went and told Jeremy about it. She had been dealt a blow by Venetia and she dealt it straight back at Jeremy. It was almost a reflex action, as if she had been given a slap in the face in a 1950s romantic comedy. Sylvia has had plenty of time to think about how she should have handled telling Jeremy that the circus was wrong. She thinks now that she should have let him be.

Sylvia has given instructions in her will that everything she has should be left to Jeremy when she dies. However, she has been trying to come up with a plan before then that will restore to Jeremy whatever identity he lost when he left the circus to please her, since she thinks she might last at least another sixty years.

When the news comes about Jeremy, Sylvia will feel so guilty that she has never made amends that she will think she is going to die of a broken heart. In a way she will be right, although it will be a very slow death, more like dying from smoking than from being hit by a train.

40

Regeneration

The Brixton Regeneration Committee has been given two million pounds by the government to spend on improving Brixton. They have spent half a million on a new shopping centre above the Tube station and they are at a loss as to how to spend the rest. An advertisement has been placed in the *South London Advertiser*, inviting suggestions for the name of a local person to be immortalized by a 30-foot statue, which will be sculpted in bronze by a local artist and placed in the small garden close to St Matthew's Church, replacing the ineffectual fountain that currently stands there.

The church stands in the middle of the one-way system that runs up Effra Road and down Brixton Hill, a grand yellow-bricked building with Roman pillars at its entrance and retail outlets on its premises, accessible from the garden. The Regeneration Committee specifies that the person should have made 'a significant impact on local and national events and should continue to reside in the area'. The edifying sight of the statue will be enjoyed by members of every strata of Brixton society, including diners heading for the vegetarian restaurant in the basement of the church; clubbers coming out of The Fridge opposite or chilling out during Mass, the regular disco held on the upper floors of the church; the happy-clappy churchgoers and the local vagrants gathering in the garden to drink Tennants Extra and mutter inarticulate abuse.

Miss Lester is reading the local press coverage of the search for a suitable candidate for the statue. She finishes the paper and then looks back to the centre pages to check the television listings. There is nothing she wants to watch. 'Well, what shall I do now?' she asks herself. Miss Lester is lonely, although she doesn't really know it. She has no experience of not being lonely to compare with her situation. Being lonely is when you sit at home at 8.30 p.m. on a Tuesday evening and say 'What shall I do now?' and there is no one to answer you.

Miss Lester takes a sheet of cream vellum paper and an ink pen and starts to compose a letter. She likes to keep herself busy. She doesn't have a wide circle of friends as she doesn't have the knack of getting on with people. The last time she can remember really laughing with someone and feeling close to them was with her mother, many years ago, before she died. Miss Lester has been terribly grateful for the attention paid to her by Mrs Fitzgerald. She has often tried to thank her for this but Mrs Fitzgerald won't hear of it. 'Violet, it is not out of the ordinary for someone to be kind.'

Miss Lester blows on the page to make sure the ink is dry. She used blotting paper when she was at school. Some thrill-seekers among the girls would steal it and put sheets of it in their shoes, saying it drew the blood from their heads to their feet and made them faint. Miss Lester wouldn't even know if shops still stock it now.

She seals the envelope and addresses it to the Brixton Regeneration Committee with a real sense of a job well done. If all goes according to plan, Mrs Fitzgerald will at last be accorded the recognition properly due to her. Miss Lester will see to it that the statue shines as brightly through the years as it does at its inception, for as long as she has the strength to wield a duster and a tin of Brasso.

41

The Race

There is a race taking place amongst the July holiday traffic on the road to Sylvia's house between three vehicles whose drivers are unaware they are competitors.

Mrs Latimer is driving hell for leather down to Sylvia's address in an air-conditioned white van, intent on finding Sylvia. Her two favourite Dalmations are travelling in comfort in the back of the van, invisible behind tinted windows. Venetia Latimer would like to drive at such a devilish speed that she burns up the motorway but her dogs get travel sick over 65 miles per hour and she cares too much for them to do it. Mrs Latimer grips the steering wheel, as menacing in her very best clothes as Cruella De Vile, although with ninety-nine Dalmations too few to fit the role.

Jane Memory, in a red sports car, is struggling against a yeast infection that is exacerbated by sitting for long periods in snug-fitting leather trousers. The Brazilian wax is starting to grow back and is causing some discomfort. Harvey, in the passenger seat, is cradling the borrowed video camera in his lap and passing the journey by filming Jane. She gives vent to her feelings of extreme vexation by making lewd gestures to articulated lorry drivers. She suspects they are all sexist pigs but many are family men singing along to sad country music to pass the journey.

Alison and Sheila, Phoebe and Boy are bowling along in the middle lane of the motorway. They made an early start and this on top of the speed of their car has pulled them nearly an hour ahead of their rivals, albeit unwittingly. They feel they are making good time on the journey so when Alison sees the sign for a service station, she and Sheila agree to stop and give themselves and the baby a break from the carbon monoxide building up in the car, sucked in through the radiator from the traffic fumes and re-cycled through the air conditioning. Sheila and Alison drink cappuccinos and Phoebe drinks uncarbonated spring water. Alison, beaming and cheerful because she received a two-pound coin in her change at the till, takes the opportunity to explain her two-pound coin rule to Sheila.

'Have you noticed, as soon as you get a two pound coin – which is something that is still unusual enough to be regarded as lucky – that you have to part with it again, usually in the very next transaction, usually at the local shop?'

Sheila searches her own purse for the coins, in case the loss of the two-pound coin at the next transaction should exert a profound change on Alison's mood, but in reverse. At an appropriate point during the rest of the journey Sheila will endeavour to find out if it counts as good luck if you pass someone a two-pound coin from the front passenger seat of a car or whether this is a rule that only holds true on retail premises.

All three use the facilities before they set off again. In motorway service stations a disproportionately high number of women who use the toilets evidently fear the transfer of venereal disease through contact with the seats. They hover unsteadily with bent knees and they wet all over the seat. Either that, or they deliberately spray their piss like he-cats because they have been arguing with their family during the car journey and they need to re-exert their authority. Whatever the cause, the droplets of urine are almost invisible on the white toilet seats and catch the unwary, wetting their thighs and branding them with a gutter smell for the rest of their journey.

Alison and Sheila, crowded together into the disabled toilet, stand shoulder to shoulder because of the lack of space. They are staring at Phoebe sitting on a white plastic potty.

'I think I ought to have her potty-trained by now. My mother said I was out of nappies at fourteen months old.' Alison is running the tap at the low sink, bending to run her fingers under the water to make a splashing sound by way of encouragement. Phoebe stares blankly back.

'My mother said I could speak perfectly formed sentences at six months.' Sheila hands a dry nappy to Alison from the bag. 'If everyone tried to match their children's milestones to their mother's proud boasts we'd be in a sorry way.'

Alison dries her hands on her trousers before fixing Phoebe up. 'You never had children, did you, Sheila?'

'No. I had Roy.'

'What will you do, Sheila, if we don't find Roy?'

'I always liked the fact that you never asked me that.'

'I don't usually ask questions unless I already know the answer.'

'I won't love him any less just because the search becomes more difficult. I am less likely to give up now than at any time in the three months I've been looking for him. With each obstacle, it just reminds me how much I love him and it shows me the lengths I'll go to so that I will find him.'

'I know what you mean because taking care of Phoebe has completely changed my life. It's made everything really quite difficult. When I got rid of my husband I swore that I would spend the rest of my life being wild and free. Now I hardly go out. Even getting to work is hard because I have to find someone to look after the baby. I used to think that the kind of person I am is made up of the things that I do. I don't do any of the same things any more but obviously I'm still the same person. I became really introspective – I think it was a kind of depression – while I tried to work out what kind of person I am if I'm not defined any more by the kind of nightclubs I go to. And through it all, I loved Phoebe more and more, because I realised what I'm prepared to give up for her – even my own sense of identity, however misplaced it was.'

'When you fall in love – and women do fall in love with their children – it is not with someone who gives you everything. It is with someone who lets you give them everything.'

Jane and Harvey are now about seven minutes' travelling time behind Sheila and Alison. Jane needs to take a rest from driving and from the trouser discomfort. She pulls into the service station, parking two rows away from Alison. Jane buys some wine gums while Harvey explores the self-help section of the book store, then she and Harvey play for twenty-five minutes on the pinball machines in the amusement arcade. They don't have a lot to say to each other since they saw Jeremy fall from Big Ben.

Mrs Latimer pulls into the service station to make a stop to check up on the dogs and refresh their water bowls. Sucking on an extra strong mint as she watches the Dalmations bound about in a wooded area near the petrol pumps and squat to pee on the grass, Mrs Latimer is unaware that she is observed by hundreds of eyes peering from behind the scrubby bushes and from among the long grasses. The hundreds of eyes belong to the whiskery faces of some of the mink, from the original six thousand released by activists, that have made it to the southeast from the south-west of England. From time to time, between fighting each other, the mink run onto the motorway, a minor hazard to the drivers who squash them beneath their wheels without realizing they have run over a living thing.

When Sheila and Alison have their first sight of the sea from the road, they call each other's attention to it and drive very fast to the nearest car park, from where they run all the way to the beach to stretch their legs.

Phoebe sits on a towel in a sundress and sun hat with factor 20 sun cream on her face, her forearms and her hands. She bangs a pink spade against a green bucket. 'This,' she says. She sips Evian water occasionally from a beaker fitted with a spout, dribbling it down her cardigan from where it slowly evaporates and joins the clouds forming over the sea, drifting back towards France where rain filtered by the mountains will be collected, treated and bottled before being sold back to Alison and other mothers. 'If I could find a way of labelling the water you spill maybe I could claim a discount next time it comes my way,' says Alison to Phoebe, sliding a finger into the baby's nappy where the elastic meets her thigh to feel whether it needs changing.

Sheila takes the grid of Roy's face from her shopping bag and she and Alison smooth the paper out on the sand and weigh it down with stones. Sheila draws a square in the sand with a stick, four times the size of the square on the paper, using a tape measure she has brought with her from her sewing kit, to make sure the sides are even. Then she draws in the lines to make a grid, using her eye to guide her.

Sheila and Alison work for half an hour to build up the picture of Roy. They take stones big enough to fit into the palms of their two hands cupped together and they arrange them in the picture; white; purple; speckled hen brown. They find coloured glass, dull and smoothed by the ocean, lying undisturbed on the beach like chunks of precious stones mined and discarded in a land where the people do not value them. They collect feathers, shells, pieces of rubber tyres.

Sheila breathes life into the picture, willing it to make a difference and bring him back to her. Let him go, she thinks. Let me have him back. Eventually, the Roy icon is finished, staring trustingly up from the beach, large enough to be seen from the sky. Sheila looks up, squinting because of the sun, then looks back quickly, bright pink dots jumping in her eyes across Roy's picture.

'Will it work?' asks Alison. They are at the edge of a path between the sand dunes, leading from the beach back to the car park. She has removed Phoebe's pink leather sandals and is holding them upside down so the sand can run out of them.

Taron, Joey Latimer and Hugo Fragrance get into Hugo's silver BMW. They are going on a driving holiday to recuperate following the long nights spent on suicide watch on London's bridges. Hugo is driving so the holiday part falls more to Taron and Joey. They have planned a route which will take in a tour of Britain's heritage sites, which they hope will be deserted, given the strength of the pound. Hugo puts the key in the ignition. Before he starts the engine, he turns and reaches into the inside breast pocket of the jacket he has thrown on to the back seat next to Taron. With a magician's flourish, he produces a water-marked, wax-sealed, signed certificate. 'This is to confirm,' reads Taron, 'that Mr H. Fragrance has purchased two hundred and fifty-five trees to be planted on his family estate in Brittany.'

'It's a reforestation deal which will net me lots of money from the EU. It will also cancel any amount of carbon dioxide the three of us care to generate over the next ten days.' Hugo turns the key in the engine. 'Let's have some fun.'

Some hours later, the holiday mood has evaporated. 'Are we lost?'

'Let's ask someone.'

'We haven't passed another living soul for twenty miles. Not even so much as a cat. We'll be lucky to see anyone, never mind asking them whether they think we're lost.'

'A cat? Why would we see a cat in a field? This is the countryside. You're supposed to look out for cows. I've seen plenty of cows.'

'Here's a sign. Let's turn in here and ask. What does it say?'

'"Paradise." That's cute. Turn in here, Hugo. There'll be someone here who can help us.'

Mrs Fitzgerald bends to pick up the second post from the mat by the front door in her office in Brixton. She has been feeling recently as if a great burden has been lifted, almost as if she can finally anticipate some good thing coming her way. She has seen madness on the buses and in the cafés of London and she knows that she is not mad. She has even been able to identify a way to prevent herself going that way, which is to avoid publicity.

She sifts through the mail. There is nothing very interesting, except for a white embossed envelope addressed in a typeface she doesn't recognize. Mrs Fitzgerald walks into her office and picks up her spectacles where they sit on her desk. She holds them so that the chain falls out of the way and brings them up towards her nose so that she can peer through them to examine the mystery envelope. It gives Lambeth Town Hall as the return address and for some reason Mrs Fitzgerald is disappointed. She sits at her desk and puts her spectacles on properly so that she can turn over the envelope and open it. It is perhaps fortunate that she is sitting down as she reads the contents.

'Dear Mrs Fitzgerald,' the letter begins, innocuously enough. 'On behalf of the Brixton Regeneration Committee, I would like to congratulate you . . .'

42

Vroom, Slam

Roy takes up the balance bar and looks along the length of the wire.

Sylvia leans against the wall of the house in a patch of sunshine near the trellis, her left foot half out of one slipper, her naked right foot moving up and down her left calf, kneading the strong muscle under the brown skin, gripping and squeezing until deep lines appear like frowns in the knuckle joints of her pink-painted toes. She taps her fingernails gently against the cup of coffee in her hand, feeling the rush of pleasure she always feels when she's watching a fellow performer try something dangerous for the first time.

'Are you ready?' Sylvia asked Roy this morning.

'Yes. I feel light.'

Vroom, slam, slam, vroom, slam. Like guests arriving late for a fabulous party, cars arrive one after the other in Paradise. Their drivers and passengers run up towards the house, stop at the arresting spectacle of Roy standing on the platform, then creep forward as slowly and quietly as if he has already broken his neck and they fear that any sudden movement will jar the bones in his body and paralyse him for life.

Among the semi-circle of spectators anticipating Roy's first step from the platform on to the high wire, a small elephant with a shimmer of gingery hair on its head, grey skin slack and wrinkling at the joints like an over-enthusiastic dieter, is testing the air thoughtfully with its trunk.

Jane Memory is there, with Jeremy's locket. Harvey has the camera rolling. They are both thinking about Jeremy. Jane is crying, her face slippery with tears. She wipes her nose with the back of her hand, the turquoise ring on her little finger catching inside her nostril and making a red mark. Harvey takes her hand, to comfort her. The silver rings on his fingers squeeze against hers and make a mild grating sound. Making a connection between the slime on her knuckles and Jane's running nose, Harvey releases her hand again quickly, wiping his own hand on the seat of his trousers.

Mrs Latimer and the Dalmations stand with the rest of the impromptu audience. Mrs Latimer is watching Sylvia.

Alison is there, fingers curled round a phone number written on a scrap of paper. The paper is wrapped round a pot of cherry lip gloss in her pocket. Phoebe's hand is in her other hand.

Sheila is standing next to them, very quiet, taking in the sight of Sylvia watching Roy. She removes the colander from her head with dignity.

Taron, Hugo and Joey have arrived. Walking softly towards his mother, watching her watching Sylvia, Joey sees that she looks as if all the colour has gone from her, even from her clothes.

A police car is coming along the track towards Sylvia's farm but no one has noticed it yet.

Roy sees Sheila's strained face among the spectators. He wobbles, then recovers. He replaces the balance bar, carefully. He understands something that has eluded him for months. He knows now that he is alive.

Alison's hand involuntarily makes a fist in her pocket,

twisting open the lid of the lip gloss with her thumb an
smearing the numbers written on the paper round it. She barely
hears the question Sheila asks as she watches Roy prepare to
step down from the high wire.

'*How could you?*'